Death at the Sanctuary

Linda Robinson

For my children, Jacey and Connor.

Chapter 1:   Loss

A Jeep Renegade trailed along a foggy country road just outside Kerrville, Texas. It was 6 a.m., almost two hours before sunrise. All the windows were down. The warm, October breeze teased Mac Williams's spiky, red hair and filled her nose with smells of cedar and dirt. With the wheel in one hand, a donut in the other, and a coffee snuggled securely between her thighs, Mac belted out the melody of *Born to be Wild* with the note precision of a pubescent boy. A dozen chocolate-covered donuts with rainbow sprinkles sat in the passenger seat ready for her to share with her boyfriend, Keene. She was about to take another bite of donut when a pair of glowing yellow eyes appeared in the path of her jeep.

"Shiii–!" was all Mac managed to say as she jerked the steering wheel right, swerving around the deer as her donut flew left, out the window, and the box of donuts tumbled into the side door. Hot coffee splashed on her thighs and Mac hissed in pain. She caught sight of the deer's fluffy white tail in the rearview mirror as it bounded into the dark, tree-covered landscape. Mac straightened the Jeep on the road. She glanced over and was relieved to see the donut box still closed. She reached over and repositioned it on the seat.

"Damn fog!" she cursed under her breath.

Mac brushed the hot liquid off her uniform khakis, the cloth quickly turning to an uncomfortable, warm dampness that clung to her skin.

"Great. Thanks a lot, Bambi." Mac continued along her route more slowly, hoping to avoid another mishap. Shortly, the wrought iron gates of Josephine's Animal Welfare Sanctuary–J.A.W.S., came into view. They were wide open.

The gates are always closed, Mac worried. She turned into the driveway and started up a hilly, dirt road that led to the main compound. As she crested the first hill, red and blue flashing lights broke thru the darkness like spotlights in a prison escape. Mac's mouth froze open.

Oh no, the lights are coming from the lion enclosure! Her thoughts quickly turned to worry about Keene, but then she reminded herself that he wasn't back from San Antonio yet. His motorcycle wasn't parked in front of his trailer when she left early this morning. She relaxed a little.

Mac drove past the small circle of buildings that made up the sanctuary's offices and food facilities, and headed towards the lights. She drove up and around a rutted dirt road. The earth was mostly dry, but she splashed through small potholes of standing water, left from weeks of intermittent rain. The county managed to barely stay beneath dangerous flood levels, which she was grateful for. The sanctuary itself was on high ground, but all roads leading in were low and flooded for hours, if not days, when the "hundred-year floods" came almost every three years.

Mac noticed that there were no sounds. No frogs, no cicadas—not one chirp—as her Jeep climbed towards the lion enclosure, the fog thinning with the slight change in altitude.

The sheriff's patrol SUV came into view. She could see Nancy, the director of J.A.W.S., yelling at Sheriff Moore in front of the enclosure. This gave Mac more worry as Nancy was always calm ... except when talking about the animals in her care; then she was as animated and passionate as a high school debate team.

Sheriff Moore was a tall, barrel-chested man, and right now he had a gun pointed at the lions. Nancy was an equally sized opponent. She was farm-girl thick, and at almost six feet herself, matched the sheriff in height.

"No! Don't shoot!" Nancy screamed at him. Nancy ran towards the sheriff as Mac saw another officer, Deputy Allen, grab her, barely able to restrain her from launching herself at Sheriff Moore.

"Stop! What are you doing?" Mac slammed the Jeep into park so quickly it lurched to a stop. She jumped to the ground and ran towards the trio. The sheriff lowered his gun and stood to face her.

"All of you! Calm down!" The sheriff shouted, his hand raised towards Mac, warning her to keep her distance. Her feet skidded to a halt.

She looked past him into the cage. Thor, the sanctuary's only male lion, had something ... no ... *someone* ... and was chewing him like a toddler with a teething ring. Mac couldn't see if the person was male or female. She could only see brown matted hair. The rest of the body was guarded by Thor's large frame. The rescue sometimes had people sneak on the property, attempting to see the lions; this crazy soul somehow managed to break into the enclosure.

"Don't shoot Thor!" she pleaded. "Are they alive? Who is it?"

"We don't think so, and we don't know. We can't get close, so it has to be shot." The sheriff yelled, then turned again, gun raised.

"Just wait!" Mac ran past him and put herself between the gun and the lion behind the fence. It was just her and Sheriff Moore, as the deputy was still occupied with Nancy.

"Move aside!" He swayed his gun from left to right. Mac swayed with it, blocking a clear shot to Thor.

"No! Just give me a chance. He's not an it! That's Thor." She raised her hands in a cautious surrender. She glanced back and saw that whoever Thor held in his paws was not moving. Thor licked him with his huge pink tongue. Mac shuddered and felt bile rise in her throat, the taste reminded her of grade school pizza. She swallowed it down and forced herself to focus on the situation.

"I don't care if it's a *he*, or an *it*. I need to get to that *person*!" Sheriff Moore's tone was irritated and growing impatient, but he lowered his gun and waited for Mac to continue.

"Just one second, *please*! Let me get something from the supply shed."

Everyone stared at the sheriff; waiting. The deputy still held Nancy, but neither of them seemed to be resisting each other. If it wasn't for the situation, they would resemble a couple in a playful embrace.

"You have ten seconds." Sheriff Moore conceded, his voice flat and his face expressionless.

Mac ran to the supply shed next to the enclosure. She threw open the door and quickly pulled out a toddler-size milk bottle from the refrigerator. She sprinted back, milk sloshing, holding the bottle in front of her like a shield. She didn't look at the body. She knew she wouldn't be able to focus if she did.

"Thor." Mac's voice was weak and shaky. The large cat did not look up. Mac cleared her throat and banged the bottle on the fence.

"Thor!" She said with authority. "Bottle!" The king of beasts looked up; blood stained his mouth as he eyed his favorite drink. Mac felt an unfamiliar pang of fear and distrust for Thor.

"That's it, baby. You see it. Come and get a drink." She tapped the bars this time. He stood, seeming to debate the decision of following her against leaving his play thing. Mac felt her eyes start to drop to the crumpled figure but quickly lifted them.

"Come on, Thor." Mac kept Thor's attention on the milk and not the person lying motionless at his feet. He started to walk towards her. She saw the gate leading to the second enclosure, the one Thor was supposed to be in, was partially open. She walked along the fence towards it, just ahead of Thor, as he followed. Mac glanced over her shoulder. The sheriff had once again focused his barrel at the lion's head.

"Please, Sheriff," Mac whispered, her eyes pleading. "Just give me one more second. He's almost there."

Sheriff Moore looked at Mac and gave her a slight nod but didn't lower his gun.

Tapping on the fence like a dinner bell, she slowly led Thor to the gate. When he reached the threshold, Thor paused reluctantly.

"Come on, Thor," Mac encouraged. "You get the whole bottle." Mac stuck the large rubber nipple through the fence wire, just beyond the gate. That seemed to be all the promise he needed. Thor stepped forward, towards his prize. Once his back legs cleared the gate's path, Nancy broke free of the deputy and pulled a lever that lowered the door with a crash. Thor's lips turned up in a snarl, and he gave an angry roar at the traitorous act.

"Thor!" Mac yelled and walked with the bottle to where his den was. She tapped on the den wall and again put the bottle through the fence. This aroused Xena, his mate, who appeared from her den and started to suckle on the bottle. With his toy behind a gate and his milk being stolen, Thor walked quickly to his den and pushed Xena away from the bottle. Mac let him take long draws of the milk before she grabbed another lever and pulled it down, lowering the doors and enclosing both lions in the safety of their dens.

Mac turned around to see Sheriff Moore, Deputy Allen, then Nancy, all rush through the first gate.

"Hello? Can you hear me? Are you okay?" The sheriff yelled as he quickly opened the second gate and made it to the unfortunate soul.

"Who is it?" Mac called out. The bottle emptied, she let it dangle by her side.

She saw Nancy cover her mouth in a silent-film gasp as Sheriff Moore knelt and checked for a pulse. Everyone was quiet. Mac kept looking at Nancy's eyes.

There was horror in them, and she kept looking from the body to Mac. A warning bell went off in Mac's brain.

When the sheriff finally withdrew his fingers, they were covered in blood. He was shaking his head.

"Who is it?" Mac demanded.

"Poor guy," the deputy said, sympathetically. "What a horrible way to go."

Mac dropped the empty milk bottle and ran towards the enclosure. When she reached the gate, the deputy blocked her from entering.

"You don't want to see this." He held her shoulders as she looked around him, then at Nancy. Nancy slowly lowered her hands from her face.

"It's Keene." Nancy barely breathed the words.

At the mention of her boyfriend's name, Mac's heart felt like it stopped.

Chapter 2:   Say It Isn't So

"No!" Mac screamed and plunged forward towards the enclosure and Keene. The deputy tightened his grip on her shoulders. She could feel his fingers press against her bones. She struggled and tried to break free, but the deputy's firm hold didn't falter.

"Please calm down," Deputy Allen said in a fatherly tone.

Sheriff Moore led Nancy out of the lion enclosure, away from Keene's crumpled body, his hand placed gently on her back. Nancy's arms were wrapped around herself in a tight hug, her head hung low, looking down.

"It can't be!" Mac screamed. She wanted to run to him ... *had* to run to him!

"I'm sorry, Mac." The sheriff closed the gate. The clunk of the metal made her wince. "No one gets in until the medical examiner and forensics team arrive," he said, looking at the deputy.

"Yes, sir," the deputy replied, still holding Mac, but not as tightly.

Nancy looked up, her eyes wide as if stuck in a scream. Mac could only imagine the horror of what she had seen in the enclosure, how it will haunt her for the rest of her life. When Mac met her gaze, Nancy turned into Sheriff Moore's big, bear-like chest and began to sob, shaking uncontrollably. Sheriff Moore paused for a brief second in surprise, then brought one arm around to comfort her.

At the whine of sirens, Mac turned. Red lights flashed in the distance. The sheriff spoke softly into his radio with his free hand, and within moments, the lights and the siren abruptly stopped.

"I've notified the ambulance to turn around." Sheriff Moore addressed Deputy Allen. "The station is contacting Dr. Anderson."

The buzz of a two-seat utility vehicle with a dump bed, the ones the workers used to get around the sanctuary, came whizzing up to the group. It was Jenny.

Jenny, with her cute little ponytails of naturally blonde hair and beautiful California sun-kissed skin, jumped from the cart. She always looked pretty, even this early. They had known each other for almost a year now, and they had become "besties," as Keene had often referred to them. Mac was never happier to see her. She broke free of the deputy's hold and ran towards her.

"What's going on?" Jenny said, looking at Nancy, then to the sheriff. "I woke up and no one was around, then I saw the lights!"

"Jenny, thank God you're here!" Mac said, grasping her in a bear hug and finally allowing herself to burst into tears. Jenny held onto Mac as she yelled to Nancy, "What the hell is going on here?"

"It's Keene. There has been an accident. He's ..." Nancy looked sympathetically at Mac, "he's not with us anymore. They found him in with Thor." Nancy's voice was shaky, but the sobs had stopped. Mac could tell she was trying to compose herself.

"What? Wait! There's no way!" Jenny hugged Mac tighter. "This is so awful." Jenny said flatly. Mac felt Jenny's gaze move slightly toward the enclosure; she said nothing more.

"Jenny." Mac said, with no response. Mac figured that just like her, Jenny was in shock at the horrible news. "Jenny!" Mac moved back from the embrace, concerned. Jenny was focused on Keene's body, what could be seen from where they stood. Jenny turned and seemed to register that everyone was looking at her.

"This can't be." Jenny looked over at Sheriff Moore. "We have too many safety protocols in place. Keene's not stupid. He—it's just not possible." Tears started to flow from her hazel eyes. "Is this really happening?" Jenny looked around. A quick nod from Nancy confirmed the nightmare. Jenny started for the enclosure; Mac hurried by her side.

The sheriff stood in front of both of them and held up an authoritative hand. "I need you all to stay away from the area."

"Why isn't there an ambulance? Why did you cancel it?" Mac asked, her sobs now intermittent, taking uncontrollable intakes of air. "Are you sure he's dead? I mean, what if you just can't tell … you're not a doctor!" She blurted out. The sheriff looked at her, seemingly insulted by the question of his judgement.

"It's Mackenzie Williams, right?" Sheriff Moore responded. Mac looked at him blankly at the recognition.

"I knew your dad in high school."

"It's Mac. My dad has mentioned you." Mac couldn't remember the stories, so that meant they were uninteresting. She just knew her dad liked Sheriff Moore.

"Good man, your dad." Sheriff Moore's face softened.

"Why can't I see him?" Mac tried to push past, but Sheriff Moore stopped her again.

"Sorry, Mac. No one goes near him 'til Bob … I mean Dr. Anderson, the medical examiner, gets here and does his investigation. I have to secure the scene."

Mac looked around the sheriff. She could only see Keene's back and make out matted brown hair that looked darker, as if wet. He was lying in an unnatural position that reminded Mac of an abandoned, mud-caked rag doll. Her mind buffered, liked an over-tasked computer, as it tried to process that her vibrant lover was the motionless figure.

"I … I have a hard time believing …" Mac crossed her arms, and uncrossed them, "that something like this would happen." She shifted from foot to foot looking from the sheriff to the deputy. Jenny went to Mac's side and held her hand, her gaze to the ground. Her supportive gesture gave Mac focus. "I mean, why would Thor attack him? That can't really be true."

"What do you mean?" The sheriff gave a perplexed look. "Lions are dangerous animals, and the gate of the divider cage was partially open."

"First, our lions were, for the most part, raised tame. Second, Keene was never sloppy with them. He understands the dangers and always followed protocol. He wouldn't even be in the enclosure without a spotter."

"Accidents happen, Mac." Jenny patted Mac's hand. Mac stared at her in disbelief.

"Keene is … was … a good employee, always followed the rules." Nancy chimed in for the first time. Mac had all but forgotten she was even standing there. "But I can't say that he was flawless. He's done reckless things before." Nancy stood with her arms crossed, reminding Mac of her fifth-grade teacher and how she looked down at the class through her glasses when she was upset. Nancy had those same thick, black glasses and crappy attitude when someone didn't follow the rules.

"What he did in the name of justice and speaking for voiceless animals has nothing to do with how he took care of them!" Mac was ticked off at Nancy's comment. "Keene is a true animal advocate, and he has done some radical acts, but he was never reckless with the animals' or people's safety!" Jenny was no longer holding Mac's hand but stood beside her and listened to the exchanges, her head moving in the direction of each speaker like a cat watching a laser pointer.

"I don't understand why he would even be in here. Did he call in on his radio?" Mac asked in a now-defensive tone. She could feel the anger and questions rising.

"There was no call, but people aren't perfect, Mac," Nancy said, turning towards the sheriff. "He could have been checking out something. The divider was open ... maybe he was checking that? It *is* unusual for my staff not to call in when coming to feed the lions, and I don't see a food container."

Mac paused, and looking puzzled, "How could the divider be open? It takes a key to unlock the safety latch."

"I'll have to wait for the medical examiner before my crew can come in and get a good look around," the sheriff cut in.

"There are two enclosures, Sheriff." Mac spoke up. "One with lions, and one without. Kind of hard to mess that up."

16

"It's dark. Maybe he didn't realize the gate was open. Nancy, can you please see to it none of your staff or volunteers come up this way without checking with us first." Nancy nodded in agreement.

"If you will excuse me, I will be right back. I'm going to see where Dr. Anderson is." The sheriff turned around and headed to his SUV.

"Wait!" Mac shouted and jogged after him.

Sheriff Moore stopped, then turned, hands planted on his hips.

"His bike. I didn't see his bike—his Enfield Thunderbird 350. It should have been up at the office."

Sheriff Moore raised an eyebrow, but his face remained composed. "It's probably around here somewhere." I'll have someone look around the property." With that, he turned and walked away. After there was some distance between the sheriff and them, Mac turned to Nancy.

"Why did you say he was reckless?" Nancy seemed taken aback by the question and placed one hand over her clavicle like an insulted Southern belle.

"Well, this is an investigation, and poor Keene is dead. I'm just giving the sheriff all the facts."

"Irrelevant facts." Mac snapped. "Keene had his crap together. He hasn't done anything for a while, and he wasn't stupid when it came to protocol."

"I'm sorry, Mac. I didn't mean it against him. This is all very disturbing, and I'm having a hard time with this too! After all, this happened at the sanctuary, which is my responsibility." Mac knew she was getting mad at Nancy because she couldn't be mad at Keene.

"I'm sorry, I just … I can't believe he's gone." Mac suddenly felt deflated and sat down quickly on the cool, damp earth. She drew in her knees and hugged them as she buried her face and cried.

Jenny went to her and held her. Mac let go of her knees and hugged Jenny back. Mac's tall, pale frame clung to Jenny's petite, brown body in an almost comical embrace of opposites, yet the strength and bond between the two seemed evident by its intensity.

"I'm heading back to the office to make some calls." Nancy said softly. "I'm here if you need to talk." Nancy lowered her head and walked in the direction of the offices. The two women sat in silence for several minutes.

"Why do you think Keene went into the enclosure on his own?" Jenny asked, breaking the quiet.

Mac wiped her eyes, looking at Jenny.

"I mean, there's no other explanation, right? He must have been checking out the gate," Mac replied as she noticed that Jenny looked scared. "I don't know, Jenny. Nothing makes a lot of sense here." Mac looked up. All the fog had disappeared. The daybreak sky was painted in soft colors of pink and blue.

"The sky is too beautiful this morning after what happened," Mac said absently, before adding, "Keene will never see another daybreak." She looked into Jenny's sympathetic eyes.

"I loved him, Jenny. I think we would have gotten married."

"I know." Jenny said tenderly as she rested her head on Mac's shoulder.

They sat and cried together.

18

Chapter 3:   Mac Gets a Clue

Mac felt Jenny stroking her hair, and it comforted her to hear the sounds of her even breaths. Neither of them tried to speak. Time froze in a horrible, long drawn out moment of pain.

Nancy walked up and gently placed a hand on each of the women's shoulders. How much time has passed? Mac wondered. Ten minutes ... two hours? It couldn't have been long. The sun was still low, but the clouds were losing their pink hue.

"Mac, you can stop now. Go to bed. You need to rest," she said tenderly.

"I can't let the animals down. I should go get the food ready." Mac wiped a tear from her cheek.

"I'll do it. You get some rest." Jenny stood and held out her hands to Mac. Mac gripped them and allowed herself to be pulled to her feet.

"I'm sorry I yelled at you earlier," Mac felt guilty for taking out her feelings on Nancy.

"I know. What happened here tonight was a horrible tragedy, and it's difficult to comprehend, let alone cope with. I don't understand it either, but we're going to need to be strong in the coming days, so please go rest." Nancy's gaze looked motherly. She drew Mac in for a hug. Nancy wasn't skinny, and she wasn't large; she was the perfect "hug" size. Mac felt secure and close to her in that moment of their embrace.

"Jenny, would you take the cart back." Nancy said, resting her chin on Mac's head. Jenny nodded in agreement and walked towards the cart.

"I'll see you in a bit, Mac." She wiped her nose with her sleeve, then got back into the cart and drove slowly towards the offices.

"Thank you, Nancy." Mac gave a strong squeeze. "Right now, I just want to go to bed for a week." Mac turned, then headed to her Jeep.

"I'm here if you need me," Mac heard Nancy call to her as she stepped up into the driver's side. Mac gave a weak wave, then drove towards the intern trailers. She had been accepted as an intern for an eighteen-month program after she earned her bachelor's in wildlife management. The sanctuary supplied a place to live and a small stipend. The pay wasn't great, but the training was invaluable for her career placement in animal conservation. She was lucky enough to share a trailer with Jenny.

Mac parked the Jeep by the offices, then walked the short distance to her trailer. She passed the small bird enclosures that held geese, ducks, sparrows, cardinals, all who wouldn't be alive if it wasn't for the rescue. They seemed curious as she passed by, their many little eyes following her.

Her feet felt heavy as she lifted them up the three small steps to the metal storm door. The door creaked as she opened it. The noise always reminded her of camping, swimming in the lake, and roasted marshmallows. The stale air in the trailer immediately assaulted her nose. She jimmied open one of the small windows and went to her room. She sat on the end of her bed, the old springs of the mattress frame crying out in protest.

A cheap mirror hung on the closet door. As she looked at her reflection, she saw that tears had cut streaks

20

through the Texas dirt on her face. She was only twenty-two, but now, as she stared into her own bloodshot eyes, she looked much older.

"Sporting some killer baggage under the old eyeballs, girl." She said to her reflection. She rubbed her face with her hands, then cradled her head. She stared into the darkness her hands made. What was she going to do without Keene? What would they do to Thor and Xena? What if they shut down the rescue? Mac pictured villagers with pitchforks and torches chanting, "Burn the lions." She knew that was an overreaction, but people tended to overreact when it came to animal attacks. Despite what had just transpired, Mac knew Keene wouldn't want any harm to come to the pair.

Sniffing her armpits in what her mom would refer to as "an unladylike gesture," Mac realized she smelled as bad as she looked. It's time for a shower and bed, she thought tiredly.

Mac reached for her dresser to get a clean pair of underwear. The small room made most objects obtainable from the comfort of her bed. She opened the drawer and discovered a blue folder lying on top of her clothes with a yellow sticky note that read:
Just giving you this for safe keeping.
~Keene

Mac's heart felt like it had stopped as she picked up the folder. Her head felt dizzy and confused. She looked around the room, half expecting Keene to walk through the door and say it was all a bad joke. She stared back at the blue folder, afraid of what she might find inside.

What had Keene gotten himself into? She sat with her hand resting on the folder. *Just open it ... you big chicken,* Mac goaded herself. *Maybe this will explain what he was doing in the lions' enclosure.*

She opened the folder and found it full of articles on the Big Bear Ranch, the hunting ranch up the road. It was owned by Clay Jones, a native Texan and good ol' boy who had both money and connections. The folder also contained a hand drawn map and notes—Keene's notes—on the ranch. The map showed houses with what looked like location and population numbers on the animals that were advertised for hunt … including Arabian oryx, Sitatunga antelope, black wildebeest, and zebras. The ranch catered to trophy hunters who could pay top-dollar kill fees. Mac picked up a newspaper clipping with a picture of Clay sitting on a cowhide chair in the lobby of his hunting ranch, with a large fireplace behind him. Mac skimmed the article. It was an interview, sparked by one of Keene's protests, on the welfare of the animals on the hunting ranch. Clay Jones was justifying his ranch.

> *"Hunting and breeding of exotic animals ensures species' survival ... We love the animals, and that's why we hunt them," Clay said in a statement to the Kerrville post. "Hunting is legal and well-regulated ... It's a more humane way to eat meat than factory processing ..."*

"Way to play the conservation card," she mumbled to herself.

Nothing in the folder seemed out of the ordinary, and it contained more of the same subject matter throughout. As she thumbed through more pages, a log sheet drew her attention. Written in the log were dates and times of Keene's visits to Clay Jones's ranch and the animals he saw there. The last entry on the log was two weeks ago.

It said, "Lion?" Mac pondered Keene's written question. Surely, he meant mountain lion. Hunting mountain lions was perfectly legal. African lions, on the other hand, were not legal to hunt in America. Mac's mind went to Thor and Xena, picturing them dead, with Clay posing on top of them like the Captain Morgan pirate, one leg down and one bent as he leans on a dead lion's head, a fat cigar clenched between his teeth in an exaggerated grin.

The last item in the folder was a blurry picture taken close to nightfall. She could tell it was an iPhone photo that had been zoomed in to the point of distortion.

"What am I looking at, Keene?" She asked the photograph. Mac saw tall grass and what looked like the shape of an animal in the weeds. She traced her finger around where she assumed the animal was.

"Wait a minute." Mac focused. She could see eyes ... a big cat, bigger than a mountain lion. A lion. She was sure it was a lion. At that moment, the trailer door banged open. Mac jumped and reactively closed the folder at the sound. She panicked, feeling like she was caught snooping even though the folder was left for her. Unsure of what to do, Mac turned from right to left in a comical dance. She opened the drawer back up, fully intending to shove the folder back in its original hiding place. There was a light tap on her bedroom door. Mac froze.

"Mac? It's me. Are you in there?" Jenny's voice floated through the door as she slowly opened it.

"Um, yeah," Mac didn't move.

"Sorry. How are you doing?" Jenny, with the door fully opened now, stepped into the room, looking at her with sad eyes and a sideways glance. "Sorry to bug you, with all that you're going through, but a fawn just came in. A volunteer cut it out of a barbed wire fence, and the vet needs to stitch a few places. I know you like to help with the fawns, and I thought it might keep you busy."

"Why the hell people can't just use wood for a fence, I'll never know. Sure. I'll go. I haven't showered yet."

Mac tried to nonchalantly put the folder aside, but just as she feared, it piqued Jenny's curiosity. "Hey, what's that?" she asked, pointing to the folder.

"Can I trust you?"

Jenny looked offended but answered, "Of course, you can!"

"It's from Keene." Mac saw Jenny's eyes open wide.

"What! What do you mean it's from Keene?" Jenny's brow furrowed, and her voice sounded off.

"Well, it looks like it's all the dirt he was trying to gather on Clay Jones and Big Bear Ranch." Mac rested her hands on the folder as if she held government secrets. "Remember how he kept saying that there was more to the ranch, but he just couldn't prove anything?"

"Yes, he would be so vague." Jenny crossed her arms. "Said he never speaks without proof. Supports that whole 'family of lawyers' crap he was born into. Damn, do you think they'll sue the rescue?" Jenny's eyes settled on the folder.

"I never considered that, but yeah, his one uncle is an ambulance chaser. That is definitely something to worry about. The rescue could lose everything." Mac was surprised at Jenny's question. She always took Jenny as a pretty, naive, sunshine-and-rainbows girl, but now Mac wondered if she underestimated Jenny. She quickly felt bad for her arrogance.

"Look at this." Mac held the folder out to Jenny. "Look at the picture. It's the last item."

Jenny flipped to the back and found the picture. She stared closely and then looked at Mac, puzzled.

"What am I looking at? I see grass."

"Look here." Mac stood next to Jenny and planted her finger on the image.

Jenny squinted, "It looks like maybe an animal ... a cougar?"

"It looks like a lion. Even Keene said so in this log." Mac whipped the picture from the folder and held it near Jenny's face. Jenny grabbed the photo and stared at it.

"Mac, I ... I ... maybe?" She shrugged. "I mean, I kind of see it." Jenny squinted. "Looks like Keene didn't know for sure himself. Look, he scribbled a question mark here."

"It's bigger than a mountain lion. Look at the head." Mac pointed to a dark circle.

"Mac, it's so blurry."

"And that around it." Mac traced her finger in a small circle around the blurred image. "I think that is a mane. Mountain Lions don't have manes, and neither do cougars, which are the same thing as mountain lions, by the way."

"Okay, first, I know they are the same, even though I don't have a biology degree like you. Second, Thor doesn't have a mane either, because they neutered him before it grew in. Third, this could be a picture of a lion on another ranch somewhere else for all we know." Jenny argued.

Mac gave Jenny an "Are you kidding me?" look. She grabbed the picture and the log from Jenny and stuffed them both back into the folder.

"Okay, okay. So—let's say it is a lion. So, what?" Jenny shrugged.

"So, what?" Mac's slapped her hands, and the folder, to her sides as she paced around the small room. "Maybe Clay owns a lion. Maybe there is more to Keene's death."

"More what?" Jenny was looking totally confused and impatient.

"I don't know, but maybe Clay is involved somehow!" Mac felt she was onto something now.

"Mac, you don't even know where this was taken." Mac took the picture back out of the folder and looked for any markers. She found none.

"Maybe if I can find his phone."

"Mac, just drop it. If it is a lion, and Keene died trying to prove it, then you need to stop. Clay Jones is a powerful man, and he's got a lot of pull around here."

Jenny looked concerned and afraid. "Besides, you have a picture that may or may not be a lion, and you don't even know where it was taken. Keene could have just had it in there." There was a moment of silence before Jenny spoke again, in a low tone. "And what if you're wrong? You don't want the attention of Clay's henchmen."

"True, Ruben and Zane are real jerks. Zane being worse." Mac remembered the many times Zane would taunt her and her coworkers at the local bars. "He always talks loudly about the hunts and brags at how they lead the animals in with food just to have someone waiting with a shotgun. Disgusting!"

"Yeah." Jenny crossed her arms and looked at the floor. "Just put the file away, and let's go hold the fawn down so the vet can work that veterinarian magic she always does."

"You don't think I should take the folder to the sheriff?"

"No!" Jenny almost yelled. The response startled Mac. "I mean, he'll just say the same thing. It proves nothing. What would it have to do with Keene being in the cage with Xena and Thor anyway?"

"Maybe he was put there against his will?" Mac could hear the wild accusation in her voice.

"Don't you think someone would have heard something? I know it's hard for you to think Keene made a mistake, but it happens. Both animals and people are unpredictable."

"You're right." Mac knew when to pretend she was done.

Jenny walked towards Mac and hugged her. "I know this is horrible, but don't torture yourself. It was an accident. A horrible accident."

"Right." Mac held onto Jenny as she felt the tears threaten to rise again. "Just when I thought I didn't have any more liquid left for tears," she sniffed.

"I'm going to head to the vet. You don't have to come." Jenny kissed Mac's forehead and headed to the door.

"Right behind you." Mac wiped her nose with her sleeve. "Just let me splash some water on my face."

Jenny turned and gave a sympathetic smile before leaving. Mac put the folder back in her drawer and covered it. Jenny's right, she told herself. You don't want to piss off a guy like Clay … not without definite proof, which I plan on getting. Mac left to catch up with Jenny.

Chapter 4:   A Lion's Defense

Mac held the fawn for almost forty-five minutes while the vet carefully cleaned and stitched every wound from the barbed wire fence he was found tangled up in. The injuries were mostly superficial, but the young deer would have to stay at the rescue for observation until he was old enough and strong enough to make it in the wild. In a couple of days, they could move him to the deer enclosure. Mac knew of a nursing mother there and hoped the doe would accept him, along with her fawn.

As Mac left the vet building, she couldn't erase the image of the tiny fawn from her mind. She pictured the baby deer, nestled alone in the crate with a just a blanket, missing his mother. The thought saddened her but he was alive. Mac knew, if it wasn't for J.A.W.S and Nancy's vision, the little guy would have died. Josephine Morgan, Nancy Morgan's mother, had started the two-hundred-acre, non-profit rescue over forty years ago. It survived on a trust fund Josephine had set up and donations. Nancy took charge after her mother passed away in 1993, and she was just as passionate and driven as her mother.

Mac admired Nancy. She wanted to follow the same path ... to make a difference ... make the world better. Her mind immediately turned to Keene. They shared the same dream and had planned to live it together.

Mac continued to a wooden rail fence that overlooked Thor and Xena's enclosure. She saw them pacing nervously in their dens, as police stood and chatted outside a yellow tape boundary surrounding the enclosure. They all seemed to be waiting for something.

The sun was making its way up the horizon. Orange and red painted the landscape, as the leaves of the Texas Red Oak and ash trees signaled the upcoming fall. Sprinkled between the brilliance of color, the evergreen cedar trees twisted and turned their thin trunks in celebratory dance. White, yellow, and purple wild flowers grew in between prickly pear cactus and long buffalo grass. Soon, the sun would be fully up and all the animals would try and escape its heat under the thick foliage or building shelters around the sanctuary. There was at least another month before real relief from the heat would settle across the state.

Mac usually liked this spot, except now it felt wrong. This was where she and Keene would stand every day. They always took time in the afternoon to talk, and breathe in the countryside. They would discuss where they were going next—perhaps Africa, to help protect the rhinos and elephants from poachers. Keene had a bigger purpose to serve, and he wanted to share it with Mac, but now instead of a future together, she found herself alone, wondering how her boyfriend had been mauled this morning. It was impossible to comprehend that she would never take an afternoon walk with him again.

Mac listened as the officers yelled across the field to one another. The morning should have been filled with sounds of birds singing, longhorns mooing, and the bleats of sheep. Instead, voices yelled orders and questions, and occasional curse words as people carelessly stepped in ant piles or feces.

"They are beautiful animals."

Mac jumped and turned to see Sheriff Moore walking up behind her. He raised his hands in a half-mast surrender.

"Sorry to startle you."

Mac thought he looked like he walked out of an old Wild West movie, in his tan cowboy uniform hat and guns holstered to his side.

"Well, of course I didn't hear you … with all this noise," Mac snapped. She felt bad for being rude, but she was infuriated with the violation of her solitude.

"You know your guys are stressing *all* the animals. This is supposed to be their refuge from people. Even we don't make a lot of contact with them, so they can live in peace."

"I'm sorry, Mac. I will remind the team, but there is a bigger picture here."

"I know." Sheriff Moore's statement diffused Mac's anger a little, and she turned back to the lions. "They are stressed. All the strange people roaming about … being kept in their dens … you can tell they are stressed by their pacing." The sheriff turned and watched the two lions walking back and forth … panting and unsettled.

"Mac, I know these animals are important to you. They weren't shot, so I'd take that as a win. Dr. Anderson and Deputy Allen will be the only people up here soon. I'd have them up sooner, but I wanted to check the gate. It seems to be working fine, and Nancy locked it."

The sheriff leaned on the fence a few polite feet from Mac. Mac considered the folder and wondered if she should mention it, then decided against it. Maybe Jenny was right. It didn't really have anything in it.

"I loved him." Mac stared absently into the distance. "I really thought we were headed to bigger things but now …" Mac's voice cracked as tears broke through her dam of composure. "We just celebrated my birthday two months ago, and he gave me this necklace." Mac pulled out a plain silver heart locket. She opened the locket and showed the sheriff a picture of her and Keene, cheek to cheek, smiles wide. She lingered on the picture, remembering how happy they both felt at that moment in time; a moment forever frozen in her locket.

"That's a good picture. I'm sorry for your loss," Sheriff Moore said. They stood in awkward silence for a moment. Mac knew he was waiting for her to compose herself, so he could ask questions. She had known Sheriff Moore since she was little.

How old does that make him. Fifty? Fifty-five? Old.

"When was the last time you saw Keene?" Sheriff Moore interrupted her internal debate.

"I saw him last night." Mac took a rag from her pocket. It was that or her sleeve. She blew her nose and took a deep breath before continuing.

"He was sitting on his bike, putting on his helmet. He said something about listening to a band in San Antonio and then partying on the River Walk. He said he'd be back later."

"Was he alone?" The detective asked.

"Yes."

"You didn't go with him, see him, or have any contact with him since?"

"No, I didn't, because I was on shift, so I couldn't go. We texted a bit, but I never got ahold of him after nine. I wasn't too worried, considering he was going to hear a band. He has friends he likes to crash with. I usually wake up when he rides in, but I didn't hear anything. I went out early to get donuts without him, and I didn't see his bike. I figured he'd be back soon, and I'd surprise him with donuts and coffee."

"I had Deputy Allen look for the bike. So far nothing." Sheriff Moore stepped a bit closer to Mac and shielded his eyes from the sun.

"So, you didn't see him at all, or talk with him? Is that usual for your relationship?"

"Sheriff, I was a little worried. I did expect to hear from him last night, but like I said, he has friends he usually stays with when it's super late. Safer that way, with the bike. The next time I saw him, he was dead." Mac glared at Sheriff Moore. "I don't appreciate you questioning my relationship, considering what I'm having to deal with right now."

"Yes. Of course. I'm sorry, but I do have to ask questions. Do you know of any issues he was having? Maybe more incidents with Clay Jones?"

Mac's temperature boiled at the mention of Clay's name.

"Clay Jones is a prick! Excuse my French. That's not a ranch he owns, it's a killing farm."

"The Big Bear Ranch is a hunting lodge. I know Clay and Keene have had their own disagreements about that. I've been called there a couple of times in the last year, as you know. Clay's put in several complaints on Keene—harassment, disturbing the peace, stealing."

"First of all, Clay stole the animal's life! If someone stole his trophy, that's no concern of mine. That beautiful animal should have been wild and not mounted on a wall. Second, no one can prove he took anything. Third, did you know he raises those beautiful buffalo for people to shoot, stuff, and mount on their walls like they took them down with their own bare hands? They just hang them over their fireplace like it was some kind of feat to shoot a half-tame, gentle animal! Clay Jones should be charged with stealing from nature, murder, and just being a greedy asshole. Too bad there isn't a law for that."

"You seem very passionate." Sheriff Moore said. Mac spun to meet his gaze.

"Do you think it's okay, what Clay is doing?!" Her hands were on her hips, and she was leaning forward.

"Personally, no. I hunt a little, but I eat all of what I kill. I'm not big on the trophy hunters. Legally, he's within limits, though."

The sheriff's honesty and straightforwardness put Mac off guard for a second.

"Ah yes, the good ole' Texas laws—people hiding behind conservation laws so they can hunt and kill what they want." Mac stood up tall and crossed her arms. "You and Clay go way back, don't you? Old high school pals?"

"I wouldn't say pals, but we have known each other since we were kids."

"I'm not stupid, Sheriff. I don't think you're a bad guy, but the buddy system is alive and well in Kerr county."

34

"What is that supposed to mean, Mac?" The Sheriff's demeanor changed to a less friendly manner.

"I'm sure you've looked the other way a time or two." Mac was pushing her boundaries. She didn't need the sheriff as an enemy.

"Why was Keene interested in Clay and not the other ranch owners? Clay's isn't the only hunting ranch in Texas."

"Keene was checking the place out." Mac said. She had another opportunity to bring up the folder but decided against it once again. "He had his suspicions that Clay had other things going on. He never told me what." A long silence fell between them. "Do you think this was more than an accident?"

Sheriff Moore looked a little shocked at Mac's speculation.

"I'm not saying that at all right now," he responded. "I am just a little curious as to how Keene ended up back here, but his motorcycle is nowhere to be found. It does leave a lot of unanswered questions. Someone might have stolen it. Tell me about the bike … pretty fancy for a rescue staff member."

"Keene comes from money, if you're wondering how he could have such a nice bike." Mac's expression gave an intended look of "duh."

She turned back to the lions. "These lions have been through so much. I don't want them to be branded as murderers. Thor was someone's pet for four years; his name was Caesar then. He was castrated, defanged, and declawed. Since he was castrated, he had no testosterone to maintain a mane, so he's often mistaken for a female. I feel like his pride was stolen from him."

"That does seem cruel." The sheriff looked at Thor. "He doesn't look as majestic without a mane. I can see how he is a victim in all of this."

"The owner found that a lion, even with all he took from him, is still a lion. He couldn't take care of Thor. First, he tried to donate him to the zoo, but zoos can't take possession of an altered animal. The zoo called Nancy to see if she could help. She was afraid of where he would end up next if she didn't take him. Even though this rescue is for native wildlife, Nancy couldn't bear the thought of worse things happening to Thor than what he had already been through. She used a mountain lion enclosure for him. Nancy can be a little overbearing sometimes, but her heart is big, and she never backs down. She's a strong woman."

"You seem like a strong woman yourself," Sheriff Moore was looking her in the eyes. He seemed to be sizing her up. Maybe he was using his police training and intuition to profile her. Mac straightened her posture and crossed her arms. She hoped her black combat boots and safari green uniform added to the affect. After all, how intimidating can a twenty-three-year-old woman look to a sheriff?

"Soon after that, we got Xena," she continued, not responding to his comment. "But not soon enough for her. She had been in a traveling circus for years. After the circus disbanded, the animals were moved to a barn where they stayed for two or three years before locals could get the city to act on the complaints of smell, noise, and animal abuse. When permission for seizure of the animals was finally granted, they found many large animals—bears, lions, zebras—all in ten-by-ten cages of filth. It was obvious the owners cleaned the cages by just spraying a high-powered hose while the animals were still inside. They were malnourished and hadn't seen the light of day in years."

"That's cruel," Sheriff Moore stated.

"Nancy told me how she cried as Xena put her paw on grass for probably the first time in her life when she moved into her enclosure here at J.A.W.S. The rescue also took in a black bear from the barn. He's still traumatized; he's not social and can't be paired with the other bears. I think sometimes I can see a little contentment when he sits in his bath. He sits in it for hours in the heat and stares at the trees. I hope he's thinking of the trees and not the past."

"Mac, I promise I will find out what happened, and if I can exonerate Thor and Xena, I will. It seems the least I can do, considering what people have done to them." Mac was touched by his words and gave a nod of approval.

"You have a good day, Mac. Thank you for your time and information. I have some work to do. Here's my card with my cell." Sheriff Moore handed her a business card with a shiny silver star symbol on it. "If you think of anything or need to get ahold of me, please call. That's my personal cell number."

"Thank you for looking into this and not just blaming Thor and Xena and thinking Keene would be so careless."

"Well, I haven't ruled out an accident or even suicide. Just haven't seen enough to say what it was."

"It wasn't suicide." Mac said assuredly. She looked into Sheriff Moore's eyes and held his gaze for a long moment.

A loud squawk from Sheriff Moore's radio cut through the silence. He grabbed his radio handset.

"Sheriff?" The voice said.

"Sheriff Moore here."

"Bob's here." The voice of Deputy Allen came across the radio.

"Roger, I'll be there shortly. Over and out." The sheriff tipped his hat in a gentlemanly gesture of good day and made his way to the scene. Mac briefly watched him walk away, then resumed her watch over the wooden rail, wondering how she was going to live without Keene. She hung her head low. She was never going to touch or see his beautiful smile again.

Chapter 5:   What a Mess

Deputy Allen stood outside the lion enclosure with Dr. Bob Anderson as Sheriff Moore walked up. Deputy Allen knew the sheriff and Dr. Bob went way back. In fact, they had been best buds as teenagers. Deputy Allen liked Bob. He was a decent fellow and funny, in a "bad, dad jokes" kind of way. He was not your typical coroner. He was a highly qualified medical legal death expert, thanatologist, and forensics consultant, which is why the county didn't need both a medical examiner and a coroner.

Dr. Bob was considered good looking. He was tall and a little thin, but he sported an unshaven look the ladies loved. He wore a black windbreaker, black jeans, and always wore black cowboy boots ... no matter what day or how hot it was in Texas. He also always carried a 1930s design, brown leather doctor's bag.

"Hey, Steve." Dr. Bob greeted Sheriff Moore. "I hear there's been a *cat*-tastrophy." He looked at Sheriff Moore and gave him a wink and a Cheshire Cat grin showing his bright white, perfectly straight teeth. Deputy Allen let out a chuckle before he could reel it in quickly enough to cover it with a fake cough.

Sheriff Moore moaned at the bad pun. "Bob, this is why you don't get second dates. Your jokes are painful. Plus, this isn't a joking matter. The Keene boy is dead here."

"Someone is always dead when I arrive, Steve. No need to get your panties in an *uproar* ... I can see the boy is *lion* over there." Dr. Bob's smile went from ear to ear.

Deputy Allen mock-coughed madly now. He was relieved to see that even Sheriff Moore cracked a smile.

"Dammit, Bob, stop."

"Sorry, Steve. Sometimes you have to find humor in life, or it will drive you crazy. Deputy, to the lion's den!" He turned with purpose and pointed to the cage like a man going into battle.

"Sheriff," Deputy Allen said as they walked. "The crew found a set of keys in the victim's pocket along with his ID card, twenty dollars, and some change. Didn't have a wallet, just stuffed it all in the pockets of his cargo pants."

"What were the keys to?" The sheriff walked alongside the deputy. Dr. Bob followed close behind.

"They were to the cage. I verified with Ms. Morgan that those belonged to the sanctuary, and only she had an extra set. They've been bagged and sent to the labs for prints."

"Good job. I think this should be easy to wrap up as accidental death. Maybe the boy was on drugs. I've seen people do worse on them."

Deputy Allen pondered the idea. "It makes sense, sir, but I've never personally seen him under the influence."

Dr. Bob passed the pair as they drew closer to the enclosure.

"Dr. Bob," Deputy Allen inquired as they walked towards the enclosure's entrance. "I can't help but ask, why do you carry that old medical bag?"

"Well, Chris, first, it's not actually old, it's expensive. It's called new vintage. It matches my nostalgic

40

humor, and it is a good conversation starter with the ladies. Need I say more?" Deputy Allen rolled his eyes as they approached the two enclosures.

"So, on your right," Sheriff Moore began, "you'll see our two suspects, Xena and Thor—mostly Thor. As you can see, they are both locked in their dens right now, for the safety of us and them. Don't want anyone accidently getting too close. Their dens open up into larger enclosures. There are two, so one can be cleaned. They were moved from the enclosure on the left—which is where the Keene boy is—to the right. It is exactly the same layout, just in reverse. They get them from one enclosure to another by that door on the pulley, in between the dens."

"Interesting." Dr. Bob looked over at Keene. "I see the Calliphoridae are already starting to gather on our poor boy over there."

"Call-i-what?" Deputy Allen gave Dr. Bob a curious look.

"Blowflies. Pesky things, but efficient. Did you know their larvae is used in maggot therapy to fight infection?"

"No, but I think I will stick to Neosporin." Deputy Allen crinkled his nose at the disgusting image.

"So, what happened, Steve? Allegedly, of course."

"Well, from what we can tell, Keene was in the lion enclosure for whatever reason. Maybe he got the enclosures confused. There are two safety enclosures. You go through the first one, which is the inner door, to the second one that leads out into the big enclosure. There's also a den that the lions can be locked in for vet care, feeding, or sleeping.

"The first to find Keene was Nancy Morgan. She said she was just walking the grounds. There isn't a lot of blood, and she said she only saw Thor licking him, not the actual attack. I didn't see a lot of drag marks either."

"Hmm, so let me get this straight, Steve. This young, animal guy went into the lion enclosure for whatever reason, then he turned to walk out, and he was kitty food?"

"I know. Doesn't make much sense," Sheriff Moore replied.

"Was he suicidal?" Bob scratched his head.

"Not as far as we know. Your guess is as good as mine as to why he'd be in there." Sheriff Moore pointed over to the enclosure and Keene's crumpled form.

"Maybe he was intoxicated or on drugs. Your tests will help with that, Dr. B.," Deputy Allen added.

"That is what keen eyes and science are for, my boy. Determining the facts." Dr. Bob paused before opening the door. "Those beasts are secure, right?" As if on cue, Thor bellowed out three guttural roars, making them all jump and take a step back. Deputy Allen walked forward and opened the door to the enclosure with a bow.

"After you." Deputy Allen gestured towards the inside, but Dr. Bob paused.

"You're sure we are good here? I'm not dressed to be someone's dessert; I would have worn red."

"You flatter yourself, Bob," Sheriff Moore commented. "Your jokes stink too much to make you appetizing." A sly smile crossed Sheriff Moore's face.

"Ouch." Bob said, grabbing at his heart. "You got me right here, big guy." He entered and got to work. Deputy Allen noticed him looking down at Keene for some time and then turning slowly, seemingly to study the surrounding area. The lions were close to the fence and watching intently.

"You watch our comedian friend, Chris ... from outside the cage. If anything goes wrong, shoot the lions," Sheriff Moore said and turned to walk away.

"Where are you going, Sheriff?"

"I'm going to take a quick look for that bike again, then go talk to Clay before anything official gets started."

"So, we are keeping this on the down low?" as Deputy Allen spoke the words, he noticed Dr. Bob turn around at this question and raise an eyebrow.

"Just a little bit. I need to get some more info."

"Gotcha, Sheriff. I've got this." Deputy Allen gave a quick, two-finger salute.

"Me as well, Steve." Bob gave an exaggerated wink, wink. Sheriff Moore headed back towards the main entrance.

The sound of a camera "click" made Deputy Allen turn. He saw Dr. Bob taking pictures of Keene, seemingly being careful not to disturb the area around the body, carefully walking in cat-like grace.

"So, it looks like he was dragged from here." Dr. Bob made an invisible trail to the right with his pointer finger. "Not very far, as Steve mentioned. I don't see any struggle marks. Could have been taken by surprise, but something isn't right. Not enough blood."

"Maybe it soaked into the ground or washed away with the rain." Deputy Allen wove his fingers into the holes of the fence, then pressed his face up to the cool, thick wires to get a closer look. His hat pushed back on his head as he looked in.

"It hasn't rained since yesterday evening. There should still be a puddle, or at least a large stain, from this type of injury. Have your people extend the search in the enclosure. Maybe he didn't die right here."

Deputy Allen nodded in response.

Dr. Bob knelt by Keene and opened his bag. He put his camera in his bag and pulled out latex gloves, putting them on with a snap as he looked closely at Keene's neck.

"I can see bite and claw marks. The ones at his neck here," Dr. Bob pointed to Keene's throat and traced his fingers over the holes in Keene's flesh, "these are deep. Had to have hit the artery." He turned and looked at the lions. "So why aren't our kitties covered in more blood?" Deputy Allen looked and saw Thor had some red staining, but nothing appeared to match the intensity of the attack.

"The left leg has also been chewed on, but by the angle of the neck," Bob paused, "the victim probably died almost instantly from a fractured neck and blood loss from the severed artery. I'll know for sure after a complete examination has been done, but I'm pretty confident that's what I'll find."

Dr. Bob now took a large meat thermometer from his bag. Deputy Allen hadn't seen a lot of dead bodies, but he knew what was next, as Dr. Bob inserted the thermometer into a gash on Keene's body, just under his rib cage on his right side.

44

"Yep. Eighty-eight point one degrees. He's dead. The sheriff was actually right on this one."

Bob turned the body and examined the skin. "Rigor is starting to set in. Lividity has settled a little on his left side—the side he's lying on. But still, not enough blood. And when was the time the body was found?"

"We got the call at 6:15 a.m."

"Huh. Interesting. So, this had to have happened at least an hour before that."

Dr. Bob slowly put Keene back in his position and stared into his half-closed eyes. He turned to looked at the lions, which had now lain down as the morning warmed. They stared back at him.

"I'd swear I just saw the big one lick its lips." Dr. Bob turned to Deputy Allen. "Hey, Chris!"

"Yeah?"

"On which day do lions eat people?"

"What? I don't know." Deputy Allen gave Dr. Bob a puzzled look.

"*Chewsday*." Bob said dryly, and Deputy Allen rolled his eyes.

"You need to stop. You're going to make me *puma* pants, Doc." Both men burst into adolescent laughter.

"You win that one my friend. By the way, go ahead and call for transport. Have them take Keene to my office for an autopsy. It's time he took a ride. His death was probably accidental, but it's always good to be sure. Plus, I'm bored. Nothing this exciting happens here."

"Right." Deputy Moore called for the wheels and mentally agreed that nothing happened in this town aside from drunken fights and spousal abuse. He was also slightly ashamed that he felt a little excited about the situation as well.

Chapter 6:   That Clay Jones

Clay Jones's cowhide-upholstered chair gave a leathery squeak as he reclined back with a fat, wet cigar between his thin lips. He usually didn't smoke until after dinner, but he needed to think and relax. His mostly salt-and a-little-pepper hair, cop-like mustache and narrow goatee gave him a charming Texan look that accented his tan face and full cheeks. He always wore wire-rimmed glasses and a buck-colored cowboy hat with silver star conchos on a leather band.

His fingers were still on the phone when he yelled to the door.

"Ruben! Get in here!" A short, boxy Hispanic man in his early thirties quickly opened the door.

"Boss?" Clay stood, hand still resting on the old-fashioned black phone as he put his cigar out in a hand-carved ashtray made of cherrywood and accented with nickel plating stamped with the Texas star. A gift from his wife. The smell of tobacco, cherry, and ash filled his nose. If Clay was anything, he was nostalgic.

"Do you know who just called me?"

"No, sir."

"Steve. Sheriff Moore. Now why would I be getting a call from him, son?" Clay called anyone who wasn't considered his equal or business partner *son*, just one of his ways to let people know who was actually in charge.

"I don't know, sir. Everything was taken care of."

"Well, if everything was taken care of, I wouldn't be getting a call from anyone concerning that Keene boy!"

"I don't know. Maybe 'cause of all that protesting. Probably just that."

"That better be all. Go and wait for the sheriff, will ya. Show him in as soon as he gets here."

"Got it." Ruben raised a tattooed arm in a mock salute and left with purpose in his stride.

"Boy's not bad." Clay said to his office walls. He sat back down and looked at all the trophy heads that covered the wall: lions, bears, elk, a giraffe, and an elephant. His eyes fixed upon the spot where his favorite head went missing. He could still see the shadow where the dust and sun didn't touch for the five years it rested on the wall. That damn hippy. I hunted that white tiger down for days. Paid a lot of money for the opportunity and almost got killed by that beast. Stupid hippy stole it. I know he did. He did it to let me know he got in here.

Clay picked up a few files from his desk and walked towards a painting of him with his boot on a slain bear's head and holding his favorite shotgun, a Remington 870. He pushed it aside and opened a safe. This ranch was old, and it had all the hiding places of an old western movie.

In the safe, where he stored all his important documents and finance logs, were a tattered, black, leather-bound Holy Bible, and three additional unlabeled files. The Bible had been passed down from his great, great, grandfather. Clay rarely read it these days. He had enough of it when he was teenager. If Clay did something wrong, his father would take a switch to him and then make him sit and read this Bible for hours. He had read all the way through it ... two times.

48

He stored his files in the safe because he didn't believe in computers or government. He didn't own a cell phone, preferring to use hand radios on the ranch. He was off the grid unless he wanted to be found. He didn't even get cable this far out in the country, so he still had an old tube TV with a VHS player attached to it.

There was a knock at the door.

Clay quickly put the files in the safe and moved the picture back in place, ensuring it was perfectly aligned on the wall. He was a stickler for ensuring everything was straight and uniformed. Crooked pictures drove him nuts.

"Hey boss." Ruben peeked his head into the door. "Sheriff Moore is here."

"That was quick. Must have called me while en route. Damn cell phones. Anyway, send the man in." Clay assumed his confident position, dropping himself back into his high back chair as Ruben led the sheriff into the office.

"Ah, Steve!" Clay stood and offered a meaty hand to the sheriff before drawing him in for a man hug. "What brings you here, you old so and so?"

"Unfortunately, business today, Clay."

"Really? Sit, Steve. Tell me what's on your mind." Clay sat, the leather making a crunching sound similar to boots stepping on fresh fallen snow. He gestured to two smaller chairs across from his cowhide throne and his expansive, walnut, hand-carved desk.

It's all about power, he stated and smiled to himself. Whoever has the power controls the room.

"No, thank you, Clay. Bad back; I need to stand."

Clay was put off by the arrangement but managed to crack a smile. "Of course. What can I do you for, Steve?"

"I'd like to ask you just a couple of questions about Keene Saunders."

"Ah, the Saunders boy. Pest. Like all tree huggers. Could have stood to cut that long hair of his."

"Keene is dead, Clay. Apparently, an accident at the animal rescue. I can't go into details yet."

"That's a damn shame. Never liked the boy but wouldn't want to see any harm come to him."

"I know he has been quite busy protesting your hunting ranch."

"Ahh, yes. These animal extremists just don't get that humans are on top of the food chain, and this is all natural. God gave us domain." Clay paused, straightening two silver pens on his desk, "He would sneak onto my property and let some of the animals free. Dangerous act."

"That was never proven to be Keene," the sheriff commented.

"Of course, it was him. He's always putting flyers on my customers' cars and yelling at them when they leave the ranch. He just doesn't get that humans aren't meant to just sit around having soy lattes and eating nothing but salad while they discuss how we should plant more trees and how life is so unfair. We were put on the planet by God to be leaders, hunters, and gatherers. God gave humankind dominion over the animals. If our ancestors sat around and smoked the wacky weed or protested all day, we'd be as extinct as the Doo-doo bird."

"Politics aside." Steve smiled, electing not to correct him on the pronunciation of *dodo*. "He did seem to be giving you a bit of a headache."

"I followed all the legal protocol. Submitted all the reports. I haven't seen the boy in over a month. So, I guess the law, which would be you, finally worked this time."

"Hmm. Yes. I did see the complaints stopped right after he was accused of stealing your white tiger head." Steve looked around at all the heads mounted on Clay's wall in a morbid parade, eyes settling on the spot notably missing a head.

"Yep. Never heard anything about my missing trophy. Anyway, maybe jail time scared him because he finally left me alone. Is there a reason you're here, Sheriff? If you could get down to business, I have a gaming tour to put together."

"Sure, sure. Busy man, I understand. I'm just asking questions. I really only have one more."

"Shoot."

"Can I have a look around the property?" Clay was stunned at the question but tried to play it calm.

"Why would you need to look around my property, Steve?"

"I'm just trying to see what Keene was doing on the last night before his accident. He's been known to visit here, so I just wanted to see if he might have come here."

Clay gave a smile. "Why Sheriff, you saw the 'No Trespassing' signs. Those signs are there for a reason. I've got big game out there. I've got mountain lions, feral hogs, and all sorts of native Texas animals that would be a danger to you. I'm going to have to politely say no to your request, without a warrant and time to get the game corralled for your own safety." Clay stood to ensure the sheriff knew the conversation was over.

"Ruben! Come show Sheriff Moore out and bring me the info on the next tour."

"If that is all, I have a business to run, it's a packed day, and I'm now behind on getting the evening festivities planned." The door opened, and Ruben held it for Sheriff Moore.

"Nice forty-four you got there, Ruben." Ruben's jacket was open as he held the door. He looked down at the gun the sheriff pointed to, holstered to his side under his jacket.

"Never go anywhere without it." Ruben patted it. "Never know when you're going to need it around here." The sheriff nodded, then turned to Clay.

"Thank you for your time, Clay." Sheriff Moore tipped his hat.

"Why don't you come back, Steve, and I can give you a decent discount on one of the hunts."

"Not my cup of tea, Clay, but thanks for the offer."

"You have a good evening, Steve." Ruben led Sheriff Moore to his car. Clay watched from the window as the sheriff drove down the long road towards the ranch entryway. Ruben returned with the paperwork Clay had requested.

"Ruben, get Zane and go take a look around the property."

"What am I looking for?"

"I don't know, but something led Steve here. Start with the perimeter. He doesn't need a search warrant for that. Work your way in. Look for any sign that Keene may have been here last night."

"Right! On it," Ruben replied and left. Clay didn't know why Sheriff Moore was here. He obviously didn't have evidence of anything, but he had something. Clay would have to keep an ear out, maybe make a few phone calls. He had an important auction event coming up and couldn't waste time dealing with a curious sheriff or nature boys—even dead ones.

Chapter 7:   Lion or Mountain Lion?

The long day had passed and the sun was finally sinking into the hillside. Mac headed back to her trailer, mulling over the last few dismal hours. The soothing coos of Eurasian collared doves filled Mac's ears as she drew close to bird housing. Three walk-in-closet-sized enclosures held various native Texas birds in one phase of rehabilitation or another. Usually, birds came to the rescue very young; fallen from their nest during a storm or windy day. Others came as survivors of pet cat or dog folly, to the horror of their owners, and the confusion of the pet as to why their new toy was taken away.

Tiny amber eyes, made more noticeable by their soft, grey, feathered faces, followed Mac as she passed a group of resting doves. Their repetitive low rhythm was replaced with the chirpy song of a Northern mockingbird, in his own enclosure due to his territorial nature. The last enclosure held sparrows. Their grey, white, brown, and black feathers blended perfectly into the dry, Texas landscape. They were Mac's favorite, because they reminded her of her grandmother. Her grandmother would feed these wild birds every day, chasing away the larger birds so that her little sparrows could eat. Her grandmother passed away over a year ago, but every time she saw a sparrow, she remembered her, along with her wonderful meals and warm hugs. Something she deeply missed and wished she could have right now.

Mac continued along the stone path, stepped up the stairs, and opened the trailer door as it gave its usual creaky welcome.

54

"Hey, Mac." Jenny said flatly as she was downing a Gatorade. She had her purse and keys on the table.

"Headed somewhere?"

"Nancy just asked me to go to the Bandera office to pick up animals for transfer." Jenny looked annoyed. The Bandera location could keep baby birds and rabbits, but any animals needing vet care were transferred to the rescue's main location.

"I really hate that drive," Jenny continued. "Probably take me close to an hour, then I have to pack the animals. And, oh my God, if Elizabeth is working, she is going to talk and talk. I'm tired, and it's going to be like three hours before I get to bed!"

"Kinda goes with the territory, right?" Mac noticed that Jenny seemed to complain a lot more than most about the work.

"Right. I know, but today's been a little taxing, don't you think, Mac? Nancy should have given us the day off." Jenny looked at Mac.

"The animals still need feed, but if you need some time off, I can ask Nancy to call for some more volunteer help."

"What about you, Mac? How are you holding it together? You lost your boyfriend!" Jenny's look was almost suspicious or judging.

"Do you think I'm not upset?!" Mac felt her temper simmer, and Jenny raised her hands in surrender, acknowledging that her accusatory tone was out of line.

"No, sorry, I'm just upset, and you're handling it better than I would if my boyfriend was mauled by a lion."

"Do you have a boyfriend?"

"Wha—? No, I was speaking hypothetically." Jenny took a frustrated breath. "I'm just tired. I need to get this done. Do you need anything or want to go with?"

"Nah, I'm going to shower. Now that the animals are taken care of, I'm going to try and process what just happened." Mac tried to soften her tone, but she was still upset by Jenny implying that Keene's death wasn't affecting her. Focusing on finding out what Keene was looking into and what might have happened was all that was keeping her from falling apart right now.

Mac walked into her bedroom, she could hear the door open and close as Jenny left. She went to her closet and swiped hangers quickly to the side, one by one, until she found black jeans and a black sweatshirt. She also rifled through a chest in her closet and found a working flashlight. She changed from her working clothes into the dark clothes, grabbed the flashlight, and pocketed her phone. Of course, the phone was useless for calls out here in the country, but she might be able to use the camera, or the light if her flashlight should fail.

Mac heard the deep grumble of the transport van. She jogged to the family room, then pushed aside the cheap lace curtains from the front window. She saw a light cloud of dust from the van in the darkening sky. Glancing at the setting sun, she knew it was now or never.

I don't have much time. By the time I reach the dirt road adjacent to Clay's ranch, it will be night, Mac concluded.

She checked the moon phase app on her phone, confirming that the moon was going to be almost full that night, and no rain. At least that was one thing in her favor.

She should have plenty of light. She knew she needed a plan of action, though.

Mac remembered Keene once taking her to a road that ran between Clay's ranch and a white farmhouse, to spy on the ranch. They were taking pictures of Clay's animals, through the wire fencing, when Ruben and Zane found them. Ruben confronted Keene, and it quickly escalated into a pushing match that ended with a broken camera and warning to never come near the property again. Keene had never taken her back with him to Clay's after that time. He said it was too dangerous, so she assumed he wasn't paying late night visits there anymore, either. Now she wasn't so sure. When they last visited, the farmhouse was for sale and vacant. She hoped it was still vacant. If so, she could probably hide her car there.

***

A half-hour later, Mac pulled off the road at the old farmhouse. She saw a tractor covered in weeds near the house, and she slowly rolled her car beside it, making it less visible. From there she walked down the path Keene had taken her on a few months ago. It went deep into the weeds and ran along the ranch's fourteen-foot-high fence. The grass was higher now, and Mac could barely make out the path. She walked along the outside of the fence for an hour, looking to see if Keene had found a way in or left anything behind, any hints that he was here recently.

The brightness of the moon allowed Mac to walk without turning on the flashlight. She saw mostly weeds and bugs, and she constantly swiped at the high-pitched buzz of mosquitoes dive-bombing her ear. When she heard a noise to her left, she quickly grabbed the flashlight and turned it on, catching a glimpse of a frightened elk. She also saw a small herd of Oryx in the distance. Their eyes glowed in the light, but they seemed more curious than scared.

Mac could make out the starting and ending points of each enclosure, and she saw some of the hunting blinds used to target animals from a safe position. Thankfully, they were empty. She wasn't sure if they hunted at night, but it was something to be careful of. The image of these beautiful animals being hunted under those circumstances sickened her. It was like shooting fish in a barrel. Hell, some of the animals were probably so tame they would eat out of your hand.

A branch snapped to Mac's right from within the fence; she froze, feeling like a deer in a hunter's sight herself. She listened, hearing nothing but the faint bleat of the other animals. Mac moved slowly forward, then suddenly felt afraid. Whether it was the realization of being alone in the dark with no one knowing where she was, or the feeling of someone watching, she didn't know.

Oh my God, what am I doing here? Her heart raced, and she heard its audible thumps in her ears, but that was the only thing she could hear. She walked a few more steps, feeling a little more confident that her fear was only in her head.

"Get a grip, Mac," she whispered. She bravely moved forward, convinced her paranoia was just that. A rustle of grass stopped her again. The feeling of being hunted returned, except this time it felt more like she was being hunted by an animal. She gripped her flashlight tightly. On the count of three, I'll turn and shine the flashlight next to me. It'll be nothing. She felt like she was being stupid, considering she could see the fence and knew she was outside of it. *One* (Mac could hear her heart again), *two* (thump, thump, thump), *three*! Mac turned quickly, shining the bright light into the grass beside her. Bright yellow eyes stared back at her.

"Aaaa!" Mac tripped over her own feet and fell backward, landing on her backside with a hard bump of her tailbone. The flashlight fell from her hand and dropped beside her.

Mac could see an outline of the deer as it bolted towards the trees. She breathed a sigh of relief. Dang it! I'm so stupid, how could I have—

A large animal ran directly in front of her, only the fence between them, in pursuit of the fleeing deer. The wind from the speed of the beast blew her hair back as it bolted by, the smell of musk hitting her face as it leapt into the trees where the deer ran. Mac was frozen in fear. What was that? That was huge. She picked up the light and aimed it in the direction of the animal's exit, but the white circle of light found only weeds and trees—nothing else.

A chilling scream, like that of a small child, came from the darkness. As Mac tried to register what she heard, the scream came again, then was cut off short. Mac scrambled to her feet and started to run. The weeds cut at her face, and she almost tripped two times as she headed back towards her car. A noise from inside the fence caused her to veer right, off the path, and into waist-high grass. She had the sensation of flying and realized her feet were not on the ground as she face-planted into the weeds and dirt.

"Ow!" Pain shot up her leg and her shin. A warm, liquid dripping sensation ran down her leg.

The fall happened so quickly; Mac still had a death grip on the flashlight. She lay there for a moment ... dazed ... and confused as to how she got on the ground in the first place. She shined the flashlight on the spot of pain. Her jeans were ripped.

"Man!" I really liked these jeans, Mac grumbled to herself. She followed her flight path backward to what she must have tripped on. Mac's breath caught in her chest. It was a motorcycle, and she was pretty sure it was Keene's. She stood and walked over to get a closer look. It was black. Yep, it was definitely Keene's.

Pain throbbed in her leg. Looking down, she saw blood staining her jeans and felt it dripping down her leg.

Mac sat and shined the light to her knee. It was a good cut, but nothing life threatening. She brushed the slightly moist dirt from her jeans and picked a pebble out of her right knee. A hiss left her lips at the resulting burn. She searched her pockets and found a bandana she usually carried to wipe sweat. This time she used it to wipe the blood from her knees. The cloth burned her raw skin. Doesn't look *too* bad. She noticed a thin peel of skin dangling from her cut. She had experienced worse and wasn't a big wimp when it came to cuts and bruises. As a teen, she BMX-bike raced and had quite a few tumbles in the beginning that had toughened her up, especially since she was biking with boys. No crying in BMX racing.

A bright light caught Mac's eye. It was coming from the road that ran along the outside of the property. Someone was coming. With nowhere to hide or run, Mac

"Good. Now forget about the sheriff. I'm going to take a nap in my room. I'll see you at dinner."

"Yeah. I think I'll take a nap too." Mac and Jenny went into their rooms, but Mac wasn't tired. She knew Clay was behind this somehow. She wasn't sure if Keene had figured out what it was and was trying to get proof, or if he was at the same place she is now. But she was sure it had something to do with his death.

Mac quietly got up from her bed and slipped out of the trailer. The sky was getting dark; thunder rumbled in the distance. I'm going to go back and take a look at Xena and Thor's enclosure, she decided. There must be something the sheriff and his crew are missing by just passing this off as an accident. The clouds rumbled in agreement.

Chapter 17:   Time to go Hunting

Crime scene tape created a large rectangle border around the front of the lion enclosure. Mac walked up to it and paused, as if alarms would go off if she disobeyed this bright yellow authoritative demand—"Do not cross." She confirmed no one was around, went under the tape, then walked up a short dirt path. She could see Thor and Xena in the second enclosure ... lying down in their dens ... enjoying the peace and quiet. Mac had a sudden image of Thor licking Keene's head. She covered her eyes, rubbing them hard until the horrible image was replaced with bright colored firework patterns on the inside of her lids.

Am I the only one who sees this doesn't make sense? Mac wondered to herself. She knew Keene would not have walked into the enclosure without checking all the safety features, and definitely never alone. I've got to be missing something, she fretted. Surely there had to be more clues as to what happened. Mac knelt and examined the ground. She had taken a class in ichnology and could track most of the local wildlife by their tracks—she also became pretty adept at following hunters and taking apart their traps behind them.

The ground was moist when the police had arrived, it was now bone dry, but held the shape of the footprints nicely. Problem was, there were tracks everywhere. Mac presumed, that since the police deemed this as an animal attack, they weren't as careful as they would have been at a crime scene. This annoyed her since there were still so many unanswered questions surrounding Keene's death. As she studied the tracks, an unusual set of shoe patterns

102

stood out to her. These prints were smooth ... like the rubber boots used when the cages were cleaned. Except the lion's area isn't due for a cleaning until tomorrow.

"Two sets. Equal distance apart." She spoke directly to Thor and Xena who were now watching her intently from their dens. She followed the boot prints all the way to the enclosure door. Her eyes strained in the failing light as Mac calculated the weight of the people.

"One person over three-hundred pounds, and the other just over two-hundred," she said aloud.

No one is three-hundred pounds that works here, and no one on the police force looked that large either. Of course, I didn't see everyone, since I went back to the trailer and cried.

"Would the coroner's office have carried him?" Mac's heart gave her pain at the image of Keene in a black body bag. She took out her iPhone and turned on the light, then swept the light back and forth at the ground, until she found tracks that looked like wheels.

"Nope. Keene was taken via gurney." She looked over at the lions who had become bored and were licking their paws. There were so many prints it was hard to make them out. She sighed in frustration.

"Ha! There you are." Mac exclaimed as she saw the same smooth boot marks leading away, but this time they were side-by-side, and they were not as deep.

If two people were carrying something heavy, like a body—like Keene's body—it would explain the weight difference. The person at his head would carry about seventy percent of his one-hundred and eighty-pound-ish frame, making a two-hundred-pound man look like a three-hundred-pound man. The other tracks look like, minus the extra weight, someone about one-hundred and fifty-pounds.

"If I were the gambling type, I'd go all in that Ruben and Zane are my Cinderellas for these rubber-boot slippers."

Mac walked up to the enclosure's gate. It was locked. She found herself caught in a memory as she brought out a set of keys.

It was last year; they had been dating for one month when Keene presented her with a small, gold gift box with a silver bow for their one-month anniversary. Inside were a set of keys, the keys she held now. He had made her copies of the keys to all the animal enclosures. He remembered how she had told him it broke her heart every time she passed the cages and saw the faces of the more domestic animals—the ones that were supposed to be wild but were raised as pets—at the edge of their cages, begging for affection. The staff wasn't allowed to pet them because Nancy's goal was to transition them back to the wild.

Mac's favorite animal was the fennec fox. He was small—smaller than a cat—with ears almost as big as a rabbit's. He was surrendered from some twenty-ish-year-old man who hid him in a college dorm room for almost a year before getting busted. The man had named the fox Fenny. Mac would whisper Fenny's name and sneak him little treats when she passed by his cage. She had always promised herself, and Fenny, that if she left, she would take him with her.

The night Keene gave her the keys, they both went and visited Fenny. She got to pet him, feed him treats, and he happily ran around them in circles. They laughed so much that night.

A smile unconsciously appeared on her face at the happy memory. Moments later, a rumble from the heavens reminded her that she didn't have much time, and her smile faded.

Mac unlocked the first gate, then opened the second. Flashes of heat lightning lit up the night, and she could see some parts of the ground were a deep red, like clay. Or maybe that was Keene's blood. Her stomach clenched in a nauseated protest at the reminder that Keene had died such a horrible death. She was so wrapped up in finding out what really happened, that she hadn't been able to process her loss. Keep it together ... for Keene, she pleaded with herself.

She noted drag marks. They weren't very long, so she assumed Keene wasn't found far from where he had supposedly died. Mac was surprised at the lack of blood. Big cats go for the neck, she contemplated. Unless Keene's neck was broken, and a tooth didn't nick an artery, there should be more blood.

The sheriff asked me about mountain lions, she remembered. Why would he do that? Unless he thinks Keene was killed by a mountain lion, and not Thor or Xena. Clay has mountain lions on the ranch. Seems risky to cover up an accidental death, but I assume the press would be pretty bad.

Mac considered calling the sheriff, but after the last conversation, she felt she needed something more substantial. The thunder was right over her now, and she felt drops of warm rain on her face. Very soon the tracks would be gone.

She took out her iPhone and tried to take pictures, but it was too dark. Only shadows and white splotches showed on the screen.

"Upgraded camera my ass."

Mac followed the tracks outward until she hit the stone. Since she had only taken one class and didn't hold a master's in tracking, that's where she stopped. She needed more evidence.

Why was Keene at the ranch? What was he looking for? He probably had more reason to be there then hunting. There are several hunting ranches in Texas ... why was he so interested in Clay's?

It wasn't right, the way Clay and his associates would raise and hunt animals just for sport, but Keene had the big picture. He believed the way to change the culture on that sort of hunting tradition was to raise awareness, and one way he did that was by talking at schools. He was a die-hard on educating the next generation; those were the ones who that could change things. So, what else was it?

A flash of lightning, quickly followed by a loud boom, told her time was up, and she started to jog back to the trailer. She passed the farm animals. She could see Bella, a large potbelly pig, taking shelter in her stall. Bella was friendly, happy, and smart. Her owners were going to sell her at a market after she got bigger than they expected. A volunteer rescued her and brought her to J.A.W.S. Bella saw Mac and ran to the fence to get her snout scratched. She just wanted ... to survive ... to be loved. She got plenty of that attention here, as well as all the apples she could eat.

The rain now let loose in a tropical dump. Life is just one big sucky mess right now.

"Dammit!"

Bella ran to her shelter and Mac ran to hers. Mac reached her trailer, soaked to the bone. She knew she couldn't show the tracks to anyone, but she was going to find out what was going on. I can't go to the sheriff. I need something solid, something that proves Clay is involved. Mac knew what she had to do. She had to go back to the ranch.

Chapter 18:   A Lion in the Hand is Worth Two in the Brush

The heavy downpour sounded like a typhoon on the metal of the trailer roof, but like many Texas storms, it left as quickly as it came. Mac opened her bedroom window and looked out. The black clouds were fading away, and night was creeping in. The air smelled fresh and cool. Cicadas were starting their nighttime song. The nearly full moon was hidden behind clouds but still managing to light the night.

I need to go back to the ranch and see if I can find proof of, well ... anything, Mac mused. She remembered the map Keene had placed in the folder. She brought out the folder, then took out the map. She paused. This is the last thing Keene gave me, the last thing he touched. Keene's face appeared in her mind, his smile, his light laughter. Then the image of Thor standing over him rushed in, causing her to shake her head violently, ridding herself of the awful image.

"No! Focus! For him."

Mac looked through blurred eyes at the map. She studied the buildings and then widened her gaze. She noticed an "X" marked along the fence line. She also saw numbers scribbled at the bottom of a page that looked like a date—tomorrow's date. She debated about telling Jenny all of this but questioned whether she would keep her mouth shut.

Jenny was acting strange. In fact, she had been for the past few months. She had become increasingly private and didn't talk much about her time off. Mac assumed she went to visit family, but why wouldn't she talk about it? Everyone had family drama. Or maybe Jenny had a secret life, like with a woman. Jenny should know she would be totally cool with that. Mac even brought up the subject once or twice hoping Jenny would feel safe jumping out of the proverbial closet, but Jenny never took the bait. Her behavior patterns remained a mystery to Mac.

Mac folded Keene's map, picked up her phone, and grabbed a flashlight. This time she planned to park further away. She knew of a little side road and an old barn where she could leave her car. It was about a quarter-mile walk to the property from there. Mac put on her black jeans and shirt, a hoodie, and high-top hiking boots. She was coming prepared this time.

"Just no fricking snakes, God!" she prayed out loud.

****

Mac had parked her car and made it to the ranch fence by 8:30 p.m. The ground, though recently rained on, had sucked in the liquid like a sponge and was sticky, but not muddy. The humidity was starting to build, and a sliver of the moon was visible from behind the clouds. This time, with Keene's map in hand, she followed a path to a location designated with an "X". Just as she figured, the "X" marked the spot where a chain link fence was cut and folded back to a small opening. It was close to the spot she had tripped over the bike. Another fifty feet and she would have found it.

She pulled the fencing back more, like a door. It moved effortlessly. Keene must have used this a lot. She squeezed through with little effort, since it was apparently cut to fit Keene's size. The map showed that this opening led to a service road. Mac trudged about half a block of waist-high grass until her boots went from ground to a dirt road. The moon was now out, giving her enough light to walk the road without using the flashlight. She didn't want to use the flashlight unless she had to; out in the middle of the country, a small light looks like a spot light in the darkness and would cause too much attention.

Mac was heading to what looked like houses on the map. Keene had circled them, but he didn't add any notes. What the hell were you doing here Keene? What could be so important you'd risk your life?

Just before she came into a clearing, she could see the lights of what she now could see were bunkers, not houses. They were curved metal buildings, painted brown. The bright light over the door drew every bug within a twenty-mile radius. Mac stood beside a tall tree and checked out the open area as a deer would a field. Nothing moved outside or inside. She quickly ran to the left side of the building. The gravel driveway screamed her arrival, but there was no one there to hear it.

She pressed herself to the side of the building and looked in the window. The glass was painted black. She went to another window, and another.

That's weird. Why paint them all black? Her head started to pound, and sweat dripped down her brow. She was nervous, and it was getting humid. She regretted the warmth of the hoodie, though she did appreciate the bug protection.

Mac continued on and made her way to the door. She felt a hard thud against her sleeve and looked down to see a stink beetle on her arm.

"Blech," she said, flicking it from her sleeve. "Gross."

More bugs pelted Mac as she entered the light of the doorway. She almost screamed as one thudded against her cheek. She could handle wild animals, but insects creeped her out. She quickly tried the door handle as she felt another bug land in her hair. The door was unlocked. She lurched inside and did the dance that every girl does when a bug is in her hair.

"Ugh! Ick, ick, ick, yuck, ick!" she jumped and whispered to herself. Mac stood in blackness, hopefully bug free. She got her flashlight out, taking care to keep it pointed at the ground in the dark hall.

"This is scary as crap, Scooby," Mac whispered to herself in a cartoon voice. She had a new respect for Scooby-doo and Shaggy. They weren't chickens at all. They were heroes for sticking with a blond, crazy-ass ghost hunter and two batty chicks.

Mac looked to her left and found a door. Opening the door, she shined the flashlight around the room and saw an old dusty desk covered with candy wrappers and magazines. She didn't bother to look around; this office didn't look used. She opened the door across from that and two more. One was a cleaning closet, whose supplies looked dry and smelled of mold and bleach; the other was a bathroom that actually had toilet paper and newspapers for reading. There were two more doors. Mac reached those back two doors and found them both locked.

"Okay, guess I can try the other building," she said out loud and quickly wondered if she was starting to talk to herself too much.

She made her way back outside and darted from one alien bug mess to the other. This building was different. When she walked through the door, a bright light flooded the hallway. Her heart practically leapt from her chest as she looked for whomever turned it on. She could hear movement and see cages at the end of the hall.

"Hello?" More rustling came from whatever was in the cages, but no one answered. The floors were polished. Paintings of animals and pictures of big safaris and hunters standing proudly over their kills of lions and rhinos lined the foyer. Mac looked closely at the familiar face of a hunter standing over a rhino. It was Clay, a much younger Clay, about twenty years ago. Was it illegal to hunt rhinos then? Mac wasn't positive, but made a mental note to look that fact up at a later time. She took out her phone and tried to take a picture of the picture. The reflection of the flash off the framed glass blinded her.

Mac rubbed her eyes with the backs of her hands, then looked around, seeing circles flash in her vision every time she blinked. The sound of vehicles approaching caused her heart to stop.

"No, oh no, no, not now," she whispered.

Mac frantically looked for a place to hide. She tried the door handles. She opened the door to her immediate left—a desk.

I can hide under that, but what if whoever it is, is going to the office? She sprinted out and tried another handle.

112

Locked!

But the door gave way and relief flooded over her. Thank God, whoever it was didn't pull the door all the way shut. She went inside and closed the door behind her. The room was dark ... no automatic light in here, but she could just make out tables with objects on them. She could hear the sound of trucks or SUVs pulling up to the bunker. Mac turned on her flashlight but covered the lens, so only a small light could be seen. She aimed it at the bottom of the tables. They were covered in long, thick velvet. She looked underneath and found some empty boxes. She moved the boxes aside and got behind them, placing them back in front of her as she pinned herself close to the wall.

Hopefully, no one will need whatever is in the boxes right now.

Chapter 19:   Snake Oil Salesman

Sitting shotgun, Clay watched as the SUV drove up
to its destination. Ruben was driving and Zane followed
closely behind. Clay was anxious to get this part of
schmoozing out of the way. As the vehicle came to a stop
an acceptable distance from the building's door, Clay put
on his best smile, then opened his door as Ruben stepped
from the driver's seat.

Within seconds, Zane drove up and parked a foot
behind them. Clay walked to the front of the building to
welcome his guests, while Ruben and Zane opened the
SUV doors. Eight Asian businessmen stepped out. They
were all in black or dark gray expensive suits with white
shirts and silver or red ties. Clay was in his western formal
attire—expensive black alligator boots, a brown suit jacket
with gem encrusted bolo tie, and a big, Texas-sized belt
buckle.

"Gentlemen," Clay bellowed. "Please come inside
before the bugs get you." Clay opened the door and
entered. Ruben ran up to hold the door and bear the brunt
of the bug attack. Zane stayed with the SUVs. Clay then
walked to the first door to his right and opened it. In it was
a lavish sitting room with a bar. Please, come inside.
Ruben will get you all a drink. I have a great 41-year-old
Glenlivet Scotch whiskey, cigarettes, and Bolivar
Belicosos Finos Cuban cigars. Relax a few minutes. Then I
will take you to see what you are bidding on."

The businessmen quietly followed Ruben into the
sitting room as Clay made his way down the hallway to the
room where Mac lay hidden. He got out his keys, opened

the door, and flipped on the lights. The room had a warm glow. All along the walls, the lights were set to perfectly display his fine prizes. Clay looked around the room to ensure everything was perfect. He saw a box peeking out from under one of the tablecloths. He walked up and tapped it under, straightening the velvet cover. Satisfied that everything was ready, he went back to the front to get his guests.

***

Mac wanted to scream when the box hit her but managed to keep her head. Sweat was pouring down her face now. It was hot. The lights were on, but she could still see nothing from where she lay; however, she could hear everything. She heard Clay walk to the front of the building.

"Gentlemen, please follow me."

Many footsteps and quiet muttering followed, though she could not pick out words, as they all approached. She tried to breath as slowly and quietly as she could. To her, her breath sounded loud and labored, but she knew she wasn't making any noise they would hear.

"Gentlemen, may I present to you ... twelve of the finest examples of African black rhino horns."

Mac's eyes widened in horror.

"Everything is bigger in Texas, my friends," he continued. Even the rhino horns." Clay let out a chuckle, Mac rolled her eyes. The group responded in polite laughter and chatter. She knew they were pleased at what they saw, even though she could not understand their conversation. She presumed they were Asian by the sound of the language, but she didn't know exactly where they were from.

Anger rose heatedly up her neck and flushed her cheeks. She wanted to stand up and yell at them. Tell them how rhinos were almost extinct, and men like them were just one of the reasons. Every part of her wanted to jump out and tell them they were horrible murderers, but what would they do with her if she did?

"As you see, gentlemen, these are all from adults. Cut all the way down. Better medicine, right, Mr. Lui." There was an audible pause, and Mac pictured Mr. Lui bowing his head to Clay. "Go ahead and inspect, gentlemen. I just ask that you use the cotton gloves on the table there. No bare hands, please. And as always—you break it, you buy it," Clay chuckled.

"How much?" asked an older-sounding voice.

"Well Mr. Zhang," that depends on whom you're bidding against. "All the horns are by vases. The items are high-priced replicas of Chinese treasures and are sold as such, each worth thousands on their own. These are what your horns will be in when they are mailed. During the auction, when I sell the antique, you are actually bidding on the horn beside it. Whatever I say for cost, add a zero for the horn, and of course you are paying for the vase as well. Your vase or statue will be crated, sealed, and sent to you via good old United States Postal Service as the replica antique. God bless America."

"What happens if it gets lost in the mail?"

"Well, Mr. Zhang, that's the cost of doing business, but I haven't lost one yet."

Yet? That means he's done this before. I wonder if that is what Keene was trying to prove. Mac's body was getting stiff and protesting the position she had now been in for probably fifteen minutes. She could hear the men pick up objects, discuss them in their native tongue, and place them back down. Mac tried to catch names in conversation—Mr. Chen, Huang, Zhange, Wu, Liu, Zhao, Xing, and Kang-Hu. She wished she could write them down, but she just kept repeating them in her head.

"As promised, we have hunt times available. Mr. Chen, your tiger will be ready after the auction, as requested. Shall we get another drink back at the ranch, gentlemen?

The group followed Clay out. He left the lights on and shut the door. Mac listened as they left the building, and after what seemed liked forever, they got in the SUVs and went for their drinks.

Chapter 20:   Run, Mac, Run!

Mac waited under the safety of the linen-covered table until she couldn't hear the hum of an engine or the crushing of rocks under the tires.

I am lying under a graveyard of dead rhinos. Somewhere, there is a tiger being prepped for death, and I have to stay hidden under here because I was outnumbered by about twelve nut sacks that don't give a damn about animal rights. Hell, I'm pretty sure they don't care about the opinions of women, either.

Mac started to overheat from being dressed too warmly and holding back her strong emotions. She moved the boxes and crawled out into the room and stood up slowly. She instantly felt free in the larger space, an elation that was quickly cut short by a sharp spasm of pain that cut down her spine. Her eyes momentarily closed in response to her body's payback at being forced to stay in that hunched position for so long. As her muscles relaxed, Mac opened her eyes.

An atrocity laid out before her. Mac was filled with horror and a deep, overwhelming sadness. Tables lined the three walls, all draped in a thick, purple velvet cloth. Another two tables filled the middle of the room. Every foot or so a horn sat on a stand, next to cotton gloves and a vase.

The horns averaged a foot or two in length. Mac walked closer to the horns and could see how deeply the horns were cut. Just as Clay had mentioned, they were cut right down to the bottom. The brutality stunned her. Horns could be cut at a length that would allow a rhino to live, but these came from animals that were butchered. If they weren't dead before they took the horn, they died shortly after from blood loss.

A haunting feeling of fear, pain, and sadness filled Mac's heart. Thirty thousand rhino left in the entire world, and sales like these bring that number closer to extinction. Her mind had trouble wrapping around why people chose to destroy and kill, rather than appreciate. She walked slowly around the room, looking at each horn and vase. The vases were beautiful and adorned with happy prints of blue birds, red and gold scenes of Asian peoples playing in the countryside or dancing, dragons, and one with beautifully ornate willows frozen in a windy wave of elegance. One looked like it might be jade; the others looked porcelain, but Mac wouldn't know a knockoff from the real deal.

Here's your treasure you idiots ... the art on the vases, not pieces of animals.

Mac put on a pair of black cotton gloves and picked up a horn that sat next to an ebony black vase with gold, green, and red colors depicting figures within an imperial court and garden; they looked to be playing a game like chess by a water fountain. The horn was lighter than Mac expected. She imagined the rhino that lost this running from some poacher, maybe her calf running with her, being gunned downed and her horn brutally removed with a chainsaw. Mac had seen pictures of poached rhinos ... a gaping, raw hole left in middle of their faces. A beautiful animal dead because of an object made of the same organic material as a human's fingernail.

Tears streamed down Mac's cheeks as she gently sat the horn back on the stand. Her sadness was quickly replaced by anger. I could just smash all the vases, and he'd have nothing to ship them with. No sale for you, Clay. But that would only delay the auction and tip Clay off. I could steal the horns, then again, I can't carry them all. No, I need to nail this bastard. I need to get the sheriff back here.

Mac took out her iPhone. Still no bars, but at least there is juice for the camera. She took a picture of every horn and vase. She even took some selfies with all the horns behind her, to prove she was there. If I make it back quick enough, maybe I can get Clay arrested before that asshole has a chance to shoot the tiger he talked about.

Mac pocketed her iPhone and headed for the exit. She turned and slowly opened the door. The hall was still empty, so she hurriedly jogged to the entrance and cracked the door to peek outside.

The warm, Texas air hit her face like a hot towel. She looked quickly back and forth, then headed for the road. Okay, I just need to get back to the car. Then I can ... her planning was interrupted as she heard the distant sound of a vehicle approaching ... fast. Mac ran from the open road towards the safety of the trees. She could see the headlights and opened up into a finish-line-paced sprint. As the light reached her, she dove for the high grass. Maybe they didn't see me, she hoped. For a moment she didn't move or breathe, just listened. An engine revved; she could hear the sound of rocks spitting from behind tires.

Mac stumbled to her feet and went deeper into a wooded area, realizing this was now a race for her life as the SUV tore down the dirt road. The ground, with divots and mounds of dirt, made her feet unsteady. Mac's foot dropped unexpectedly into a hole, but she caught herself from falling and managed to free her herself without breaking an ankle or loosing stride. She could hear the vehicle quickly gaining on her, but knew it wouldn't fit between all the trees. Hopefully, that would give her an advantage.

The once bright moon was covered from sight by clouds, and the darkness made it hard to see. Mac could barely make out a side road that led to an enclosure. The SUV had sped up ahead and was now turning onto the road. Mac ran to the gate. Like the lion enclosure at J.A.W.S., two gates led into the main holding area. The outer gate had a padlocked chain wrapped around the door and the fence. I can get through that. I'll have better chances with a wild animal than whoever is in that SUV. She pulled on the gate and was able to squeeze through the opening. Whoever put the lock on the first gate wasn't worried about locking the second gate. She opened the second gate and sprinted inside just as the SUV pulled up.

"Wait! Stop!" Mac heard a male voice and fear gripped her heart. She ran faster, through bushes and grass. Leaves cut at her skin like razor blades as she plowed through, using the tiny bit of light the moon still offered from behind the clouds as a guide.

"Goddamn it! Stop!" The voice more commanding this time. Was that Ruben who was yelling? Zane? She wasn't going to stop and see. If I keep heading towards the moon, that will eventually put me at the perimeter. I can climb the fence from there. Let's just hope whatever is in this enclosure is harmless or full.

Chapter 21:   The Hunt is On!

Ruben watched as Zane jumped from the SUV and ran after a figure they saw disappear into the woods.

"Goddamn it! Stop!" Ruben could hear Zane yell as he disappeared in the trees for a few minutes, then came walking back to the truck.

"I can't make out who for sure, but I know it was that "Mac" girl. Only person I know with short red hair," Zane said anxiously. He was pacing in small circles with his arms over his head. "What the hell do we do now, man?" He looked at Ruben through the driver's side window.

"She ran into an active enclosure." Ruben said flatly. "A dangerous one at that." My life is in a downhill roll, he thought. It's getting deeper than I like. It'll be time to bail soon if it gets much worse.

"Hey! Dude!" Zane snapped his fingers in front of Ruben's face. "Wake up, man. Now what?"

"Grab the rifles. We're going in," he replied flatly. Ruben turned and reached for a gun from the backseat. The feeling of cold metal filled him with primal bad-assery and confidence. He picked up a ham radio from in the truck. "Texas Godfather, this is Desperado. Copy."

"This is TG. What is it Desperado? Over."

"There is a white rabbit in cage ten. Repeat. White rabbit in cage ten. Over." Zane looked at Ruben with a confused looked and mouthed the words, "White rabbit?"

"It's code for hippy trespassers." Ruben saw the *aha*! moment in Zane's exaggerated smile.

"I'm ten-eight to your location. Find the rabbit. Over."

"Right. Over." Ruben looked at Zane. "Time to rescue a nosey damsel that got herself into distress." He opened the door and hopped out as gracefully as a bear jumping from a tree stump.

"Aw, man! Are ... you ... freakin' ... kiddin' me?" Zane dragged the words out as if giving the words space would convince Ruben of their importance. Zane reached and grabbed the other gun. "It's dark. Just let her go. They can come find her later. It's her fault; she's the one trespassing."

"No, we don't need another death. Boss doesn't want any more attention. I don't want any more attention, either. That enclosure has the same mountain lion that killed Keene. Time to go hunting and get in there and get her out. Boss wanted that cat shot and burned anyway, in case of evidence in his stomach."

Ruben started towards the gate at a brisk pace. Stopping to get keys from his pocket, he fumbled with the lock and dropped the chains to the ground. Zane stood behind him.

"You good?" Ruben could see Zane was having doubts by the troubled look on his face.

"This is getting too real. I just wanted a job that made enough cash for me and Tater Tot to get the hell out of Texas, maybe settle in Florida."

"Are you serious?" Ruben laughed. "Florida?"

"Never mind. Damn it. Last time," Zane said under his breath. Ruben opened the gate and Zane pushed by him, opened the second gate and ran ahead.

124

"I can see this is going to be all me!" Zane let out a chuckle. Ruben took after him at a full run. He started to get close. Zane, seeing this, laughed again, then seeming to draw energy from the night, took off like a GT Mustang in a road race. Ruben was strong, but running was not his forte. He felt his larger frame clomping along, his breathing getting heavy. He had started too fast, too soon. He felt sweat drip down his face.

Ruben could see Zane slow and turn his head to see if Ruben was behind him.

"Man! You okay?" Zane sounded concerned as he slowly jogged backward.

Ruben stopped, bent over at the waist, hands on his knees, gasping for air.

"Yeah," he struggled with choosing between breath and words. "You go ahead ... yell ... when you ... catch her." Ruben waved towards the woods. "I started out too fast. Just need to catch my breath, then pace myself."

"Right, fat ass!" Zane yelled, and started running again. Zane jumped between the bushes and disappeared between the trees, laughing at his own joke.

"Aw man, I'm dying," Ruben said to the night. He gave one bigger inhale and choked out a meaty phlegm ball. Feeling like he could finally breathe, he headed into the woods. He jogged more slowly this time, his breath steady as he found his pace. The only sound he noticed was his feet cutting through the brush. This is too quiet. I don't even hear Zane.

A rustle on his right caused him to jump comically to the side.

"What the hell! Zane? Is that you?" He stopped, raised his gun and aimed it at the noise. "Zane? If that's you, you'd better say something before I blow your head off." The trees rustled again. Another sound filled his ears, and it was loud and coming fast! A rabbit broke through the bushes as a bright light tore through the brush. Clay came flying through the trees on his four-seater ATV, nearly hitting Ruben's head.

Ruben yelled and fell backward. His rifle went off with a loud bang as he hit the ground. The shot echoed in the still night, sounding like five rifles instead of one. Ruben was on his back, gun pointed skyward, surprised at his new horizontal view of the world. He could see the stars in the breaks between in the clouds; even the moon had come out to mock him. The sound of an ATV motor filled his ears as headlights quickly became brighter and closer. Ruben shielded his eyes.

The motor stopped; the light was blocked by a large silhouette.

"What the hell are ya doing, boy?" Clay said as his shape came into view with his hands on his hips. "Are you trying blow my head off?"

"Sorry. Lost my footing." His heart was starting to slow from a what felt like a million beats per minute to just a hundred. Goddamn, I think I'm going to have a heart attack.

"Git up, boy! Where is Zane? He has a rifle, I hope. Who are we chasing?"

"You got here quick, Boss." Clay extended a hand to Ruben and helped him stand up. "And yes, Zane is armed. He should be fine." Ruben brushed the grass and
126

soil from his pants with his gun-free hand. "We think it's Mac."

"My luck has been bull-crap, lately." Clay remarked, as if his luck was the only luck not going well. "This isn't good." Clay's brow wrinkled into several angry lines. "We need to get her out of here. Let's go."

"Dammit. These are my good jeans," Ruben complained as they walked back to the ATV. "How did you find me?"

"Well, it wasn't hard to find where you guys went. Doesn't take a master tracker to see all the broken branches. A bull in a China shop would make less of a mess." Clay stopped and looked at the moon. It had fully emerged, the clouds now on their way east, leaving behind a clear night sky. "At least we have some light, but so does that damn cat."

The two quickly went to the ATV. Ruben hopped in the passenger side, put his gun between his knees, and buckled up. It was going to get bumpy, and he didn't feel like hitting his head.

"Wonder why she is here. Maybe hippy boy told her something." Clay cranked the key; the engine roared to life.

"There was only the one time he could have seen the lion, but if he had any proof of the auction, we would have had an official visit by now." Ruben was sure of this. He knew people at the police station, and none of them had mentioned anything.

"Yeah. Guess we'll find out. Hold on!" Clay yelled as he put the ATV into drive. The engine gave another mighty roar and spit dirt and rocks from its wheels as they catapulted back into the woods.

"There." Ruben yelled and pointed towards the trees with his left hand, his right gripped to the cold metal bars of the frame, trying to keep his body stable and his head from banging onto the metal. "Branches are broken!"

Clay aimed the ATV in the direction of Ruben's finger.

"Just hope we get to her before the cat does." Clay yelled over engine. "I don't need another dead body on my hands."

"Cat should be fearful of all this noise." Ruben yelled back.

"He's hungry." Clay shouted louder. "I haven't fed him any because I was going to put out bait for his shooting tomorrow. We interrupted his meal on that poor boy so he's still hungry, and now we know he's not afraid of humans."

Chapter 22:   Did You Hear That?

A sharp cramp shot through Mac's gut. She wrapped her arm around her stomach to dull the pain. Mac willed herself to keep running, even though all she wanted to do was sit and rest. *I should reach the fence soon, just a little further,* she encouraged herself.

Remembering an old cross-country running trick from high school, she raised her hands over her head until the twist she felt in her stomach loosened. Her hiking boots felt heavy, and the uneven ground was exhausting to run on. Branches and leaves sliced at her hands. Her arms were protected by the hoodie, but it was hot. Sweat dripped into her eyes, stinging them, causing them to water and blur.

Mac was relieved to see a clearing ahead. She broke through a wall of weeds and into a campsite. She could see the outline of a fire pit and a deer blind in the trees. *I could rest up there ... maybe find my direction out of here and see if I can get cell reception.*

Mac heard a rustle in the bushes to the right of her. She froze, tilted her head towards the noise and listened as her eyes scanned the foliage ... nothing moved. Her eyes went wide as she heard a shot fire, then the distant hum of an ATV.

They are coming and it won't be long before they make it here.

Mac took out her cell phone from her jeans pocket. A bright screen confirmed her fears. Still no bars, no signal, no help. Mac looked towards the ladder and the deer blind. She figured she might get a signal a few feet up.

A stick snapped in the bushes ahead of her.

"Who's there?" she whispered as she realized she was most likely in an active enclosure with a dangerous animal. Despite the heat, she felt goose bumps and the hairs on the back of her neck prickle. Mac knew she was being hunted. She slowly headed for the ladder and the tree. Remembering guidance from a park ranger training class, Mac slowly raised her arms above her head, trying to look tall, and moved at a deliberate pace. She felt like an orangutan walking to the base of the tree. It took all her nerve to slowly climb the wooden boards. She looked behind her, but nothing was there.

I'm probably just being paranoid.

Mac's head peeked over the wooden platform and she saw only a cot and table. She pulled herself up, sat at the opening dangling her legs, and listened—she could still hear the ATV, but no other sound. She let out an exhausted sigh of relief and brought her phone back out.

Yes! Two bars.

A loud cracking sound from below startled her. She quickly pulled her legs up and lay flat to the floor, clutching her phone to her chest.

"GODDAMN IT LADY! Come the hell out!" Mac stifled a scream as Zane barreled through to the clearing. She slowly peeked over the opening and could see the top of his sweaty blond head. He paced in a circle, waving his arms in exaggerated gestures.

"What the hell do you think we are going to do to you?" Zane spotted the tree and the ladder. "Ha! I know you're up there. Just save us all a lot of hassle and come down here."

Mac would seriously consider this if it were anyone but Zane. She was tired, hungry, scared, and just wanted to give up on this whole thing.

"Alright! I'm coming up!" Zane slung the gun he was carrying over his shoulder and ran to the tree. Mac scrambled for her phone. She held it out towards Zane like a shield.

"Stop!" Mac looked over the opening. I'm going to call the police!" Zane smiled at her.

"There you ar—" A huge flash of gold sprung from the bushes.

"Look out!" Mac yelled.

Zane's blood-curdling scream filled the night air as a cougar slammed into him and ripped him from the tree. Man and cat rolled until they stopped with Zane on his stomach, the big cat mounted on his back, claws dug in to hold his prey down.

"Ahhh! Get it off!" Zane screamed as blood soaked his shirt.

Mac watched the cougar try to bite Zane's neck, but it couldn't get a good angle because the shotgun barrel was in the way. The cougar kept clawing and snapping; Zane kept screaming.

I have to do something. Mac looked for something to throw. She looked at the phone in her hand. "Dammit," she said, hesitated, then launched the phone at the cat's head. The cougar looked up, hissed at Mac, but did not let go of his prey. Mac swung her feet around. She was going to have to get a rock or a stick. She didn't like Zane, but she wasn't going to watch him die, either.

The ATV flew through a wall of branches like the General Lee in the *Dukes of Hazzard*. It landed with a skid and turned; headlights focused on the bloody battle. Clay jumped from the driver's side, grabbed a rifle from behind the driver's seat, flipped the stock into his right shoulder, and racked a round into the chamber in one smooth, experienced motion. The cougar had been startled off Zane by the duo's arrival and was backed against the tree, hissing in fear and anger at the interruption.

"No!" Mac yelled, reacting at the scene that was being laid out before her.

A single shot echoed through the woods; the cougar slumped.

Ruben jumped and ran beside Zane, gun in hand, keeping his eye on the motionless cat.

"I think it's dead!" he yelled to Clay.

"Of course, it is. I don't miss."

"Oh my God, I'm bleeding! Oh my God. Oh my God." Zane called out.

"Quit pissing around, and stop this bleeding!" Clay screamed. Ruben put down the gun and rolled Zane over. Zane screamed in agony. Mac could see blood soaking his shirt.

Clay ran to the ATV and returned with an old blanket.

"Here!" Clay threw it at Ruben. Ruben caught it and dabbed the wounds like a woman putting on cover up. Mac rolled her eyes. "I'm coming down! Don't shoot! I can help."

132

Mac climbed down the wooden boards and plopped next to Zane; hand extended to Ruben for the blanket. Ruben shot her a hard look, then gave it to her.

"The wound is deep in the shoulder," she said.

"No, really?" Ruben replied.

Mac felt a pang of guilt as she pressed the makeshift bandage into the deep puncture wounds.

"Dammit woman!" Zane screamed. "That hurts like a mother!" Mac turned to Clay.

"Do you have duct tape?"

Clay quickly went to the ATV without a word, retrieved the tape and handed it to Mac. Ruben helped her lift Zane to a seated position so she could duct tape the blanket and his arm down tight. Mac focused on Zane, not meeting Clay or Ruben's gaze.

There was just enough tape to finish securing the blanket as Zane passed out. Her mind wandered back to Keene as she realized the fear and pain he went through when he was attacked. She had to shake her head to wash away the grizzly scene her mind made.

"Let's get him in the ATV, now!" Clay ordered. Ruben and Clay supported Zane up into the vehicle as he went in and out of consciousness. Mac was relieved not to hear screaming but terrified she might see a person die. After the men put Zane in the ATV, Ruben stayed with Zane, and Clay walked back to Mac.

"Are you going to kill me?" Mac asked in all seriousness.

"I ain't no murderer. Your man got himself killed just like Zane almost did. You've caused a lot of trouble.

You should have just minded your own business. Now let's get this boy to a hospital before he bleeds out."

"Do I have any choice?" Mac met Clay's eyes.

"No. And if Zane dies, it will be your fault."

Mac remembered her phone. She quickly looked around.

"What are you looking for?" Clay immediately looked where she was scanning.

Mac didn't answer.

There it is!

She spotted the phone by the tree, then quickly ran over and grabbed it from the ground. She pressed and held the side button and one of the volume buttons on her iPhone until the Emergency SOS slider appeared. She dragged the slider to the right, and it immediately started to dial emergency services. Nine-one-one glowed on the screen as it began dialing.

Thank you, God!

Mac stared as the phone announced, for too long, that it was dialing, then Clay's thick hand snatched the phone from hers.

"Hey!"

"You'll get no signal here," he said as he killed the emergency call. Ruben is going to take Zane to the hospital a lot quicker than EMS can respond." Clay pushed the home button and stared at the screen. The camera app was open. Clay slid his thumb right to see the latest pictures.

Clay looked up from the phone. "You won't be needing this." He put the phone in his pocket. Mac knew he'd seen the pictures she took.

134

"Give me my phone back!"

"Get in the ATV before Zane bleeds out." Clay didn't wait for her before he turned and walked quickly back to the vehicle. She followed and climbed in the front seat. Ruben was tending the unconscious Zane in the back.

"You should have just minded your own business." Clay said, repeating his previous statement.

"I know what you have. You are a murderer!"

"I didn't kill them. Besides, those are just African cows, missy. Don't tell me you don't eat hamburgers."

"First of all, you're an accessory to the crime; second ... I'm vegan." Mac crossed her arms and stared at Clay.

"Hmph, figures." Clay responded as he started up the ATV. He put the stick shift into drive, and the ATV lurched forward.

"Keep the pressure on the wound." Mac yelled behind her.

Ruben gave her a "no duh" look.

Chapter 23:   Caged Animal

Mac bounced and jerked around as Clay drove the ATV at breakneck speed over the uneven ground of the enclosure. Relief flooded her body as the gate came into view. Mac looked back at Zane. He was pale, but his eyes were open.

Mac was aware that if Zane dies, she will be partially at fault, as she is the one who ran into the enclosure. I should have gone to the sheriff first. But if I wouldn't have come, I wouldn't have found the horns. What do I do? Her exhausted brain had no answer.

"Ruben, get Zane to the hospital," Clay ordered. "I'm going to take Miss Mac here to see Tony." Ruben glanced at Mac with an emotionless face. Mac dropped her gaze.

Clay took the gun from the side of the seat and tilted the barrel toward her. "You stay here, missy," he said.

Ruben and Clay helped Zane onto the passenger seat of the SUV. Clay mumbled some words to Ruben, that she couldn't make out. The SUV's engine revved, and bright headlights broke through the night as Ruben drove off. When the gravel dust cloud settled, Clay was staring at Mac.

"So, missy, since you are such the animal lover, I got a friend for you to meet."

"Who?" Mac felt like she was looking at a character from a Wild West movie. Clay, sitting there with his cowboy boots, shiny buckle, and shotgun gave her an uneasy feeling.

136

"Tony. You'll like him. You can keep him company for tonight."

Clay got back into the ATV and started it up.

"Who's Tony? What does he want? What do you mean *tonight?*" Mac yelled over the loud engine.

"Don't worry about it. He's right up your alley."

Clay drove back to the road, past the building where Mac found the rhino horns. It was less than ten minutes before he pulled up to another hanger-like building. Clay stopped the ATV in front of the doors and cut the motor.

"All right. Let's go." Clay pointed the direction to the door with his gun. Mac led the way, her head filled with images of running and taking the chance Clay wouldn't actually shot at her. But the trees weren't close enough for cover.

"What are you going to do with me?" Mac stopped walking, as if to demand an answer from the man with a gun. "Are you going to kill me?" Mac tried to act calm, but inside she was terrified.

"The cougar could have done that," he said and nudged her with the barrel. She walked up to the door. It had a keypad lock, one of the "newest" things she had seen on the ranch. Clay stepped in front of her and quickly hit six numbers. A loud click signaled the door had unlocked. He held the door open. "After you."

"Oh, now you have manners?" Mac grimaced. She walked in and motion-triggered lights lit up the middle of the hangar. It was a long hallway with cages on each side.

As Mac walked down the hallway, visions of Stephen King's book, *The Green Mile*, flashed through her mind as she passed each animal's holding cell. She was surprised to see a zebra, an antelope, and an enclosure where the resident was probably sleeping in a crate. She also saw an empty cage, about the size of a small bedroom. Panic seized her as she realized the cage was for her.

"Oh, hell to the no! You are not locking me up like one of your animals!" She turned as if to walk back out and saw the dark holes of the double-barrel shotgun.

"Step in there, Miss Mac. It's just until the auction is over. Then you and I can come to an agreement."

"And just why would I agree with anything you have to say?!"

"Well, let's just say I will be more than generous. It'll give you a chance to save more animals and leave town. Plus, you have no proof of what you saw tonight. It'll be your word against mine." Mac realized Clay was absolutely right. He had her proof—her phone—in his pocket.

"What makes you think they won't believe me!" but Mac knew the answer.

"I'm an important contributor to the economy of this town ... they'll believe me over a hippy." Clay gave a cocky smirk that she wanted to smack off his face. "Even if they don't believe me, they will back me."

"There's a bucket in the corner, if you need to relieve yourself. I'll get you some TP and some food and water. Later, Ruben will make sure you're comfy." He pointed to the corner of the cage. "There's an old blanket you could use to rest on. It's probably covered in hair and might smell a bit, but you seem to be okay with animals. You're going to have to stay here the rest of tonight—

138

maybe tomorrow—but Tony there in the next cage—will keep you company." Clays head tilted to her right. Mac turned and jumped back as she stared at a tiger in the adjacent cell, perched on top of what looked like a wooden "big cat jungle gym."

The tiger wasn't moving ... just staring intently at her. Mac shivered but couldn't help being mesmerized by his beauty.

"I knew you'd like Tony." Clay laughed as he shut the cage door. Mac jumped when the lock engaged. She could hear him moving items around in a supply closet. He reemerged with toilet paper, a battery-powered lantern, chips, beef jerky, and a bottled water. He squeezed the toilet paper roll through the bars, turning it into an oval rather than a circle. The chips crunched in protest but made it through without busting. Clay held out the jerky. Mac crossed her arms and stared at Clay.

"Right. Don't eat meat." He put the stick in his pocket and passed through the lantern and water.

"That should last you 'til the morning." Mac walked up to the bars and gripped them in her hands like a convict.

"You are really going to leave me in here?"

"Yes. I really am. I'm going to have my auction, and then you can go. I'm not an animal Ms. Mac." Clay smiled.

"No. No, you're not. That would be an insult to animals."

Clay's smile faded. "Don't poke the bear, missy."

"You murder animals!" Mac yelled, feeling anger rushing through her as she remembered the sight of the horns in the room.

"It's not the same. They are animals; we are people. Survival of the fittest. God gave us dominion over them."

"We were given intellect to be better, to take care of the earth and her creatures." Mac saw Clay turn to walk out. "Don't you dare leave me here!" Tears of anger started to stream down her face, which angered her more.

Clay turned around. Mac felt hope as he walked up to the cage. He clicked on the lantern and set it in front of the cage. He looked at Mac with a sad expression, turned and headed to the door.

"You bastard!" Mac screamed and pounded her palms on the bars. Tony jumped down from his spot and paced quickly back and forth in response to Mac's outburst.

"I'd be a little calmer if I were you. You'll upset Tony ... and stay away from those bars." Clay opened the door and let it close by itself with a click of the lock. After ten minutes, the main lights shut off. It would have been pitch black if it weren't for the low light of the lantern and the reflective glow of amber from Tony's eyes.

Chapter 24:   He'll Be Coming Around the Mountain

It was about thirty-five minutes to the Methodist Emergency room in Boerne, Texas. Ruben drove the winding back roads with the skill of a race car driver. Zane groaned and whimpered from the passenger seat. Ruben looked over and saw Zane's eyes were open, and he was conscious again.

"Man, I have to call Tater Tot and tell her what happened." Zane spoke and breathed through the pain, like a woman in labor.

"You're going to be fine. I don't think we should call anyone until after the auction."

"What-eve. You're being paranoid." Ruben saw Zane reach into the opposite pocket of his now "good" arm. Zane pulled out his phone, hissing in pain.

"Dammit dude!" Ruben grabbed for the phone. Zane texted as fast as he could before Ruben managed to snatch the phone out of his hands.

"Ow, man!" Zane shouted. "Watch the arm!"

"Ha! Got it!" Ruben dangled the phone just out of Zane's reach. Zane looked annoyed, then his expression changed and confused Ruben. He saw his eyes widen and realized Zane wasn't looking at him, he was looking at the road. Ruben turned and saw the yellow sign with a black arrow warning of the very sharp turn they had just entered way too fast.

"Hold on!" Ruben over compensated left, then right. Zane screamed like a small girl in a horror flick as the seat belt must have dug into his wound. They both slid dramatically to the right as the phone flew out of Ruben's hand and onto the floor by Zane's feet.

Ruben felt his balls descend back from their hiding place as he loosened his grip on the wheel and took his foot off the accelerator.

"Just watch the damn road." Zane hissed again at his shoulder which had started bleeding again, turning the cloth even more red.

"I would have if you hadn't been texting."

"Frickin' douchebag!" Zane yelled.

Ruben looked back at the road while Zane whistled a cuss word and bent to find his phone.

"Hey, man, sorry. We just need to get through this next day, and we won't have to worry about money for a while."

"You think I don't know that? Clay better pay good for all the crap he's put us through—double for me, now!" Zane's fingers reached his phone. The light shown bright in the truck as he looked at the shattered glass.

"What? Dammit! The screen is all cracked up now. What else can go wrong?" Zane put the phone in his pocket. "Why did you have to take my phone? Tater Tot won't tell anyone. She's my girl and just as much into all this as us. Hell, she could get into trouble for withholding information or some *Law and Order* lingo crap like that."

Ruben didn't disagree. She was in just as deep. He didn't really trust her, but she'd do anything for Zane.

"Women love a man with cool scars. What's cooler than surviving a mountain lion attack? We can even say you punched it in the face. You'll always get laid with that story." Ruben smiled at Zane. They both broke out into hysterical laughter, and then Zane moaned in pain.

"Aw, Big R. I needed that." Zane was relieved to finally see city lights. "I'm feeling woozy."

Ruben looked over at Zane with worry. Even though they weren't close, he guessed he loved him on some sort of brotherly level, or maybe he just felt sorry for him. Ruben didn't even know about Zane until after their father died. Ruben's mother had already passed five years before with cancer, which was good, because hearing about the affair and love child would have killed her. However, Zane had a crappy life. Apparently, his stepfather frequently reminded Zane he was a bastard child. He also had a favorite pastime of beating on him and his mother. So much so, he ended up in foster care for a few years, while his mother dulled the pain with drugs and alcohol. For this, Ruben felt obligated to help him out once in a while, as his life had been charmed compared to Zane's ... and to make up for his father's transgression.

"Hang in there. Hospital is coming up." Ruben began to run excuses for the attack in his head. "Let's just say way we were in the enclosure setting up for the hunt and the cat gotcha. You punched it in the face, and I shot it. That's all."

"Sounds good to me. Let's get me some drugs ..." Zane's words trailed off, and his head bobbed slightly.

"Zane?" Ruben gently nudged Zane, who was slumped like a passed-out drunk. Ruben knew the exhaustion and blood loss were taking their toll. "Hang on buddy. You'll feel better soon." Ruben said as he sped up.

Chapter 25:   Zane's Anatomy

Grace Jones stood in the Kerrville Hospital emergency room breezeway, one hand on her voluminous hip, debating on having a cigarette. She was head nurse and eleven years from retirement. Her shift was normally filled with small-town injuries. Chastity Hill's teenage boy came in earlier with a broken leg from a dirt bike accident, and Sam Steeves, Senior, brought his middle-aged son in for catching a fishing hook in the side of his head. She remembered last year it had been Sam, Senior, in for a hook in his arm. Either way, they both had no business near fish, poles, or hooks.

With the darkness outside, Grace could see her refection in the emergency room doors. She shifted her size twelve, tall frame and looked at her messy hair, absently grabbing a hair tie from her pocket. She pulled her barely long enough, dirty blonde hair tight behind her head. She could pull off a mean Nurse Ratchet look when she wanted too. Bright headlights came into view, breaking her vanity check. A white truck quickly pulled into the circle. Grace recognized Ruben's truck and headed towards it.

What broken bone or head stuck in a bucket case will this be?

Grace knew Ruben from way back in school. She was probably one of the few people who liked him ... really, really liked him. They always seemed to have a good laugh when they were together. He wasn't laughing now, though. After he parked, Grace saw Ruben race around to the passenger side and open the door. A young man was slumped over in the seat. Grace couldn't see exactly who it

144

was, but knowing Ruben, it was probably his sidekick, Zane.

"Zane! Wake up, man." Ruben shook him gently but firmly.

"Wha—? I'm fine." Zane tried to get out of the truck with his seat belt still on.

"Hold on, man!" Ruben yelled, obviously annoyed.

"You hold on! I want drugs! This hurts like a mother."

Grace reached the truck and could see the blood-soaked blanket duct taped around Zane.

"Resourceful work. What happened, Ruben?! Did he get shot?"

"Gracey… no, he was attacked by a cougar." Ruben said calmly, as he helped Zane out of the truck.

She loved when he called her Gracey.

"Oh my God. Don't move him," Grace said placing a hand on Ruben's. "You stay here!! Let me get a stretcher. We need to keep his feet up."

"I don't need a stretcher; I need pain meds!" Zane's stumbled out of the truck, and his legs gave out from under him. Ruben caught him and tried to prop him against the truck.

"Wait here, while I get help." As Grace jogged away, she could hear Ruben say something to Zane about liking the way her body jiggled when she jogged. She blushed and ran for a stretcher and help.

Grace was met at the door by Mike and Andrew, two male nurses who must have seen the truck pull up. They all joined each other and quickly brought the stretcher to Zane.

"Here, here! Mike, get him on here." Grace gave directions to the nurses. They were able to get Zane onto the stretcher and through the doors. Ruben followed behind.

"Get Dr. Wilson; we'll probably have deep lacerations, though I won't know till I cut the bandage off. I'll need saline, IV fluids, and antibiotics."

"Right." Mike answered, and Andrew nodded. The two jogged up ahead.

"We need a tetanus shot, and Doc will probably want to start rabies," Grace yelled after them.

"What the f–f–f—? Rabie-e-e-es? Zane was groggy, but conscious. "I just want drugs and schleeep."

Zane disappeared into the hospital on the stretcher. Grace turned to Ruben.

"I think he'll be okay. The fact that he is talking is good. You can fill out some paperwork in the lobby."

"Hey, Gracey, I have to get back to the ranch. He's on Clay's payroll, so he's covered."

Grace's eyebrows raised. "You're going to leave him?"

"Well, he's not going to die, and I don't want to hear him scream again when you start cleaning out that bite. I also have a dead mountain lion I have to account for back at the ranch." Grace gave him a disapproving looked. Ruben smiled back.

"Or are you just keeping me here for your company?" Ruben asked. In response to his question, warmth filled Grace's cheeks as she quickly turned around.

"Get out of here, you big flirt. I'll see your pal gets good drugs, but you need to come back and fill out the paperwork."

"Thanks Grace. You're a peach." Ruben jogged back to the truck, and Grace headed to the automatic doors.

"Hey Grace!" Grace turned to Ruben.

"Zane is a private kind of guy, so no visitors. I'll give his family a call—'less he flatlines or somethin'—then you can." Ruben winked and gave another smile Grace wished she could wake up next to.

"Go!" Grace gave a pretend annoyed wave, then headed into the hospital to tend to her patient.

Chapter 26:   Tony and Me

Mac sat with her back solidly against the far wall, staring across at Tony, who was staring back at her.

"I don't know whether to be fascinated or scared," she confessed to Tony.

Tony remained statue still. She knew he was sizing her up, looking for an opportunity to pounce on the prey before him. Mac felt she was in the presence of a magnificent, beautiful, dangerous beast.

"Hey there, big guy." Mac said softly to the statuesque tiger. "You are probably wild, scared, and hungry." She looked around to see how safe she was. "Tell you what, I'll just stay about a foot from that cage of yours, in case you feel like reaching through, but I'm going to get a little closer. I've never been this close to a tiger." His eyes were on her now—hypnotic—and she couldn't help hearing the voice of Kaa, the snake in the *The Jungle Book*, telling her to go to sleep man-cub or in this case, woman-cub.

Mac slowly scooted to the middle of the cage. She could see the tiger tense. Mac knew a little about tigers from her training, and she let out a tiger-like chuff; a tiger's greeting.

"*Tssfffftt.*"

Tony looked at her.

"*Tssfffftt … Tssfffftt.*" Mac repeated. To her elation, Tony relaxed, twitched his ears.

"*Tttffffsstttt,*" he answered her back with his own chuff,

"That's right big guy. I'm your friend, and I need to figure a way to get us both out of here," she said to Tony's amber eyes.

Mac realized her heart was beating fast in her chest. A natural response to being so close and talking to a wild tiger for the first time, she told herself. She took a couple of deep breaths to calm down. She smelled his musty urine; it burned her nose. After the fifth deep breath, she could feel her heart beat start to slow. As if in response to her new state of mind, Tony lay down on his side.

"Tony. May I call you Tony?" The tiger licked his furry lips in response. "I will take that as a yes. We sure are in a pickle. You're waiting to get shot by some egotistical businessman with an inferiority complex, and I'm debating on peeing in that bucket. This is not a good situation." Mac stretched and folded her arms over her head.

"In fact, let's sum this up. Keene died at this ranch … attacked by another big cat. Perhaps you know him?" Mac paused. Tony didn't reply.

"Maybe not. Anyway, he was here because he figured out Clay was hunting big game like yourself. What Keene didn't know, is that Clay was dealing in illegal rhino horn trade too ... or he might have ... I guess I will never really know." Mac sat with her legs crossed, elbows on knees, resting her chin in her hands.

"I got a picture of the horns, but I managed to lose my phone by throwing it at the cougar that was attacking Zane; now Clay has it. I don't have any proof, and I might have gotten a man killed—I hope he's okay." Mac looked at Tony, he was watching her while resting on his side.

"*Tssfffftt*," she chuffed at him again.

"*Tttffffsstttt*," he chuffed back.

"This takes me to the clear and present danger. I'm in a cage, next to you, Tony. No offense. Waiting to be set free … if I'm set free. Which probably won't be until after all the evidence is gone." Mac's heart felt suddenly very heavy, and her body felt weak and tired. "There is just no way to get out of this cage." Mac looked to the bucket and decided she could hold it a bit longer. Then she looked at the blanket Clay had pointed out. She slowly got up, picked up the blanket, then gently shook hair and dust from it. She sneezed several times in response.

"I'm sure Jenny will notice I'm gone," Mac told the Tiger. "She'll figure out what I've been up to. She knows me. She'll tell Nancy and someone should be here by late morning." Mac laid the blanket on the floor close to the opposite wall, so that her back could rest against it. "Yes, Jenny will figure it out. She'll get the sheriff. I'm sure of it."

"Well, we are pretty much screwed until then. For right now, I'm exhausted. Let's talk later, shall we?" Mac took the blanket and folded it like a sleeping bag, then crawled inside. It had a dog-bed-like smell and was still coated in animal hair, but it was warm and better than nothing. She snuggled close to the cold wall. She presumed it would be hard to sleep with a tiger staring at her, but exhaustion from the long night caught up to her and allowed her to quickly fall into a deep, black sleep.

Chapter 27:   Tater Tot

Zane had spent the last two hours hooked up to an IV, having his wounds debrided and flushed, getting shots and stitches. All he really wanted was to sleep.

"Here you go, Zane," Gracey said and handed him a small paper cup of pills. "Your reward for being such a good patient. It will help you sleep."

"Oh, thank God!" Zane snatched the pill cup from her hand, grabbed the water, and drank it all in two huge gulps.

"Whoa, slow down." Grace said but didn't motion to stop him. Zane felt satisfied and the cold water felt good on his throat. He wondered how much blood he lost?

"The doctor wants you to stay at least a day, just to make sure you don't get an infection or have any nasty reactions to the vaccines."

"That is fine by me," Zane said and settled back deep into the pillow. I need a break from the ranch anyway ... and dead bodies, big cats, and feisty redheads.

"Okay, well you have a sleep. I will be back in about an hour to check on you." Grace turned down the lights and left.

Within five minutes, Zane's eyes felt heavy. Whatever Gracey had given him worked good and fast. He finally felt like he could sleep. As a haze started to settle over his mind and his vision blurred, he focused on the quiet of the hospital—the beeping of machines and hum of lights. He heard the sound of small footsteps on the tile floor approaching, stopping at his door. His eyes had been closed, but he managed to peek them open just a bit. Zane smiled at his visitor.

"Is this a dream?" Zane slowly slurred. "Tater Tot! How'd you know I was here?"

"Jelly Bean! Your text. You sent me some cryptic text about bleeding and a hospital and—oh my god! What happened to you?" Jenny ran over to Zane and held him gingerly.

"Don't worry, I'm fine. I just got into a fight with a big cat."

"What! Oh, Jelly Bean, that's awful! You could have been killed, like Keene!"

"Shhhhhhh, Tater." Zane's speech was sounding more tired and becoming slurred. He whispered in Jenny's ear. "We don't want to talk about that here."

"Oh, sorry. But no one knows. Everything is fine." Jenny said, as Zane felt his eyes grow heavy and close.

"Ahhhh … uhhhh, Mac knows." Zane felt like he was starting to float, and Jenny was a dreamy angel.

"What? What does Mac know, Jelly Bean?"

Zane felt Jenny grip his arm tight, but her words were quiet and distant.

"Zane … ZANE!"

"Hmmm, what?" Zane forced his eyes to open slightly, then discouraged by their weight, he closed them again.

"Where is Mac? What does she know?"

"Mac is with Clay. She was snooping around. I don't want to go to school today, Mom." Zane trailed off again.

"ZANE!"

"HEY!" shouted a loud voice behind Jenny. "What are you doing here?"

"I … um ... I'm a friend," Jenny stammered.

"Well, it's late, and there are no visiting hours now. You are going to have to leave."

"But ... but …" Zane heard Jenny's protests and was able to peek through only one eye to see Grace shooing her out of the room. He didn't have the energy to protest.

"You can come back at visiting hours; they are from 8 a.m. to 9 p.m.," Grace said, standing in the doorway.

"Tell Zane that Jenny will be back later, please."

"Sure, you got it," were the last words Zane heard before a deep, drugged slumber took over.

Chapter 28:   Wish You Were Here

It was nearly 5 a.m. when Jenny drove up to the trailer she shared with Mac. Her stomach felt like someone let a million butterflies loose. Panic and stress gripped her in anticipation of either Mac knowing what happened to Keene and her part in it, or Mac not being there and being at Clay's ranch instead. I'm not sure which is worse, she thought. If Zane is actually right, and it wasn't the drugs, Mac is in serious trouble. Jenny parked the car and went up the steps.

She opened the trailer door quietly. The lights were off.

"Mac?" Jenny called out. "Mac, you here?" Jenny turned on lights as she walked through the trailer. She gently tapped on Mac's bedroom door.

"Mac?" Receiving no response, she opened it. The bed was empty.

Her cell phone rang. Jenny jumped, then scowled at the screen as the caller ID glowed with the name Uncle Joe, a contact she had purposely mislabeled. It rang again. Jenny let it ring one more time before answering.

"Hello."

"Jenny, there's been an accident." The Texas accent was unmistakably Clay Jones.

"What do you mean?"

"Your man had to go to the emergency room."

"What! Zane's hurt?" Jenny lied.

"He was attacked by a cougar—seems to be a lot of that going on here—but he's not hurt bad. And I want you to wait a couple of days before you see him."

154

"I can't see him? Why?"

"Of course, you can ... later. Also, I need you to do something for me, darlin', and I will be sure to compensate you." Jenny hated his sickening sweet patronizing tone.

"What? Your last favor had me break the law. You had Zane ask me for that key to the lion enclosure. I didn't know you were going to drag a dead body in there! Let alone someone I actually know!"

"Whoa, whoa, whoa! If you had been doing a better job at playing spy, maybe we could have caught Keene before he got attacked." The comment stung.

"You can't blame that on me!" Jenny was mad at the guilt Clay made her feel.

"I can. That's what I was paying you for. To keep an eye on him and tell me what he was up to." Clay's voice was cold and accusatory.

"Right. Like I could have worked and followed him around twenty-four hours a day. So, what do you want?" Jenny said bluntly.

"Well the whole reason your boy got mauled is he was trying to get Mac out of an active enclosure. She's fine, but I need you to act like you don't know where she is."

"What do you mean? Just where is she?"

"If the sheriff stops by, I just need you to play dumb and act worried about her. In fact, tell her boss, Nancy, she's missing. Tell her, in about an hour, or whenever you would normally be up for work. The sheriff will start to suspect Mac. Give me some time to close up some loose ends."

"Do I need to be worried about Mac?" Jenny definitely felt worried now.

"Mac is fine. She's in a nice, big empty cage. No harm is going to come to her. Well, unless she gets stupid and gets too close to Tony. I just need some time to talk with her. She knows too much, but I can make her a financial offer she can't refuse."

"That's bull!" Jenny's outburst surprised even her. "Who the hell is Tony!"

"Excuse me?" The irritation in Clay's voice set off all kinds of warning bells in Jenny's head.

"Why does she get a payoff? Zane's in the hospital, and what about me?"

Clay's laugh made Jenny cringe. "Why, little lady, Mac hasn't done anything wrong. You've given two men a key to hide a body, you've been spying for me for about a year, and your carelessness not only got Keene killed, but got your boyfriend attacked because you're not even a good spy!"

Heat rushed into Jenny's face and so did the feeling of helplessness and betrayal.

"You and Zane will get your money. I need to give Mac enough to keep her mouth shut for all of our well-beings. I'm thinking of all of us, darlin'." Jenny felt hot bile burn at her throat as Clay turned himself into the good guy.

"What makes you think Mac will take any amount of money?"

"Everyone has a price, darlin'. Once Mac knows she can do more good than not, like save some elephants or something, she'll take the money."

"Why do I need to stay here? Why can't I see Zane?" Jenny had a feeling something bigger was going on, and she wanted nothing to do with it.

156

"I can't have you going to the hospital and the sheriff seeing you. He may tie you to me and start asking questions. Look, Mac missing will draw suspicion away from all of us. She'll be fine. I will let her go in a day or two. The police will have nothing. Work there another week or two, then quit if that is what you want. I don't need you there anymore," Clay finished.

Jenny didn't reply.

"Alright, missy. You got some time for a little more shut eye if you want. Don't worry about Zane. I will make sure he's taken care of and let you know when you can see him. You just do your part." There was an audible 'click' before Jenny could say anything else.

Jenny sat stiffly upright on the end of Mac's bed. I'm done with Clay. Mac doesn't deserve to be treated like that.

Jenny looked at the clock. It was nearly time to start feeding the animals. Okay, first I will let Nancy know Mac isn't in her bed, she planned. Then, I'll finish my shift and sneak up to the ranch when it gets dark again. I'm going to get her out of there and then I'm getting the hell out of this backward, Andy Frick'in Griffith of a town.

Chapter 29:   The Visit

Zane woke to an uncomfortable tapping on his forehead. Through blurry eyes he managed to make out a tactical green and tan uniform.

"Wha … what the hell, man." Zane made a feeble attempt to swat Sheriff Moore's hand away.

"Well, hello Sleeping Beauty. Looks like you had a heck of a day, huh?" The sheriff's large smile and shiny badge came into view.

"I've had better." Zane answered, as he pulled himself to an almost sitting position. "I'm a little tired Sheriff; mind giving me a break? I've had a bad night." Zane could make out Nurse Grace standing in the doorway. As his eyes focused, he could see she looked annoyed and worried.

"Sheriff, he has been through a lot, and it's very early. Couldn't you come back later?"

"Oh, this will only take a minute, Grace." Sheriff Moore aimed a charming smile at her. Zane noticed it seemed to disturb her more than settle her.

"Sheriff," Grace's hands rested on her wide hips. "I really must insist for the health of my patient."

"I'll tell you what, Grace, you go get a doctor who can tell me why he can't answer some questions, and I will leave." She looked at the sheriff suspiciously, then back at Zane. He hoped his pleading eyes would save him and convince her to stay.

"I'm going to do just that. Zane, I won't be long," Gracie said with authority and walked quickly away. The sheriff slowly re-aimed his sly smile back to Zane, who felt wide-awake and nervous now.

"You know what I hate, Zane?" Zane slowly turned his head from side to side in response.

"I hate being made a fool of. I know there are things going on around here, and as long as I know people, for the most part, are staying within the law or not hurting anyone, I tend to just let good old country boys do what they do. Know what I mean?"

Zane nodded.

The sheriff walked closer to the head of the bed and looked Zane's wounds over slowly. "Isn't is a coincidence that the Keene boy died from being attacked by a lion, and a few days later, you get attacked by a big cat too. I feel like I should buy a lottery ticket. What was it that got you?"

"I don't really know. It was dark." Zane licked his dry lips.

"Hmmm, yeah, dark. What happened? Wandered into an active enclosure?"

"Just walked into the wrong one. Got confused. As I said, it was dark. Now if that's all you have to ask, I'd like to get some sleep."

"Yes, of course, how rude of me." Sheriff Moore turned to walk away, then slowly turned back chuckling. "You know what really gets me?" The sheriff hooked his thumbs into his pockets and didn't wait for Zane to answer. "That brilliant, crazy, pun-dropping nut of a doctor ... I'm referring to Dr. Bob, the medical examiner ... well, he thinks it was a cougar that killed Keene." Zane stared at him, he felt his lips purse tight, then licked them to relax again.

"Is that so, Sheriff."

"Ayah, he sent the hairs off for DNA testing ... just to confirm, but I betcha that it won't just be African lion hair they find."

"Look, I don't know what you're getting at. Why don't you stop jerking me around, and let me get some sleep?" Zane barked. He was tired of this game. The sheriff walked to Zane's charts.

"Reading the notes on your chart, seems it was a cougar that got you too," the sheriff picked up the charts and showed him, like he could read it from the end of the bed.

He's just trying to scare me, Zane told himself.

"I can't help think how strange that is," the sheriff said tapping the chart. "Like a coincidence, you might say."

"That's news to me. I passed out. What difference does it matter what got me? That has nothing to do with Keene being attacked by lions." A voice inside Zane's head warned him he was talking too much to the sheriff.

"Oh, so you knew about the attack?"

"Word travels fast, Sheriff." Zane felt his body temperature rise, like he was facing the sun in July, standing in front of a lit grill. He could feel sweat start to bead on his upper lip and tried to nonchalantly wipe it away with a sniff; grabbing a tissue from beside his bed.

"Just saying. You know I would hate to find out that there is anything going on at the ranch besides people walking into cages full of man-eating cats, of their own free will. I'm not going out of my way to look for wrongdoing, but I'm sure as hell not going to ignore it when I see it." They both heard hasty footsteps approaching and looked at the door. Grace walk in with a very frazzled-looking doctor.

"This is Doctor—" The sheriff raised his hand and cut Grace off.

"Thank you, doc, for stopping by. I was just leaving."

"Oh, okay, is there something you needed though, Sheriff?" the doctor said, and Grace glared at him.

"You know, not right now; I've been told your patient needs rest." The sheriff looked at Grace, and Zane saw her face flush. Zane watched the sheriff leave and looked for a phone, saw one on the bedside table, and reached for it.

Zane hisses as he felt a sharp pain, like scissors had just been pushed through the skin of his shoulder. He instantly grabbed the bed railing, willing it to subside. The doctor and Grace responded quickly.

"Now just lie down and relax. You've had some deep puncture wounds but nothing life threatening. It's going to be sore, and we did our best, but you are going to have some scars."

"Yeah, thanks doc. Could you just hand me a phone?" The doctor handed Zane the room phone. Zane looked the putty-pink plastic object as if the doctor had handed him a puzzle box.

"What in the hell do I do with this?" Zane picked up the handle of the push-button phone. The buzzing of an open line called out the phone's handset, an annoying reminder that it needed a number, and it needed it now, before it made an even more annoying, broken sound.

"This is a damn toy. Where's my phone?"

"Give this gentleman a hydrocodone," the doctor ignored him. "That should make him comfortable enough to sleep a few hours."

"Yes, sir." Grace left, presumably to retrieve the pills, then the doctor left with a wave and a promise to see him in a few hours before his shift ended.

"Yeah, thanks a hell of a lot, doc." Zane called after him as he stared at the buttons. He remembered his phone was in his pocket, but his clothes were probably in the wooden locker across the room. "Dammit." It an instant, Ruben's number miraculously came as a digital picture in his brain and he punched the numbers into the phone before he lost them.

"Yeah?"

"Hey, Ruben, it's me."

"Oh, hey! I didn't recognize the number. How are you feeling man?" Ruben replied.

"Wha ... yeah ... hurts like a mofo ... listen, the sheriff was in asking questions."

"What? Did you tell him anything?" Ruben's voice was laced with concern.

"No, I didn't say, but I think he knows something." Zane could hear Ruben breathing.

"What? How?" Ruben asked.

"Man ... I just know, he said something about not looking for trouble, but not ignoring it either. Also, he said the medical examiner knows a cougar killed Keene. They are getting DNA, man!"

"Calm down. Even if they discover it's a mountain lion, they can't prove it was from here."

"What about the cat?" Zane's brain started to work quickly through what evidence could link them.

"The cat's dead and I'm feeding most of it to the pigs. The rest I will burn. Don't worry. I got this." Ruben's voice was confident. Zane lay his head back on the pillow and stared at the ceiling.

Zane could hear Grace walking up and talked low into the phone. "Gotta run man. Don't get us thrown in jail. I'm too pretty and you're getting too ugly." Zane hung up and grunted as he put the phone on the table beside him.

"Get your call in, Zane?" Grace helped him steady the phone on the table and passed him pills with her other hand.

"Yeah."

"Here, you just take these and rest. I'll see to it the sheriff doesn't bother you on my shift again." Zane swallowed the pills and lay back down. Grace turned out the lights and left.

"I'm screwed." Zane whispered to the walls that were now starting to blur. A pleasant euphoric sensation swept through him as the sweet sleep that only prescription drugs can give took him over.

Chapter 30:   Back at the Ranch

Clay poured himself a large scotch and emptied it in one gulp. He didn't usually drink this early, but he needed something to take the edge off. He walked over to the office window and sat in his favorite chair. It was his dad's. The smell of old leather and cigars surrounded him as he pictured his dad, sitting quietly, looking out over the ranch. Back then, the ranch was only a cattle ranch, and money had been tight. They had struggled during the eighties.

His dad passed at forty-nine years young. Being the only boy among three sisters, Clay took over the ranch and the debt. After hearing some tourist brag about shooting a zebra at a ranch nearby and how much they paid, he decided to quit the cattle farming business and go into exotic game hunting. He kept a few cattle for the tax write-off on the land, but big money was in shooting game.

Trophy hunters paid top-dollar kill fees to hunt exotics. One African antelope, with a trophy fee was worth $35,000, paid for the entire herd's food for the year. Business was booming, but with the good came the annoying. Clay started to receive a slew of hate mail from people who were appalled at the idea of legally killing exotic or endangered animals, but without him, he reasoned, the animals would be extinct. In the beginning, he wrote back to everyone who had something to say, letting them know it was the hunters that mostly supported the financials of wildlife conservation, and without them, some wild animals wouldn't exist at all.

Some stopped after the first letter, but others, convinced of Clay's crimes against the animal kingdom, continued to play a tennis match of paper to pen ethics. In the end, he stopped writing. He didn't care what other people had to say or what they believed. He was getting customers and cash; that was all that mattered.

Why, I'm doing the world a favor and making a buck in the process ... God Bless America.

Clay justified to himself that he was all about doing things the right and legal way, except for the rhino horns, and the occasional lion or tiger he smuggled in for a hunt. The profit on the horns was too ridiculous not to do it, and he'd stop when the rhinos became extinct. That's just survival of the fittest, he would argue to himself. If not me, some other rancher will make a profit off it.

Clay didn't realize he was dozing until a knock at the door jarred him awake.

"Hey, boss. Got a sec?" It was Ruben calling from the other side of the door.

"Come in." Ruben walked in looking like he'd been to war. He still had blood on his jacket from Zane's cougar battle, and his eyes were bloodshot and tired. Clay gestured to the chair in front of him.

"You look like something the cat dragged in," Clay said.

"Yep. It's been a hell of a night. I mean morning, now." Ruben replied flatly. "What's the plan boss? With Mac and the auction?"

"I want to get those horns out of here before someone comes looking for Mac."

"So, what are we going to do with her? If you are going to let her go, she'll run straight to the authorities."

Clay was amused and let out a deep guffaw at his question.

"What would you have me do? Kill her?"

"Well, the rhino horns? Keene? She's going to say something."

Clay laughed again. "Oh son, you have to know what makes a person tick. I'm sure I can offer a deal she can't walk away from. And once she agrees, she'll be involved, whether she likes it or not."

Ruben paused, then finally spoke again. "Okay, but what if she says no?"

"She'll say yes. Trust me. I'm going to offer enough money that she'll be able to save her rhinos, or gorillas, or whatever the hell she wants. She's smart ... she'll take it. Besides, it's her word against mine. The rhinos are already dead. She has a chance to save live animals. She'll take it, trust me. They all do. Now we have work to do. Let's get prepared for the auction so we can get this stuff off the property." Clay noticed Ruben had crossed his arms and was contemplating something. It made Clay feel uneasy.

"I know this has been a rough two weeks. Expect some extra in your paycheck for appreciation." Ruben's arms lowered.

"How much?"

"If this sale goes off without a hitch, you'll see an extra twenty grand."

166

"How much is Mac getting?" Ruben had a look that Clay didn't like and felt his own face turn into a deep frown.

"Mac will get enough to keep her quiet, which will keep you out of jail. Want to put a price on that?" Clay stood and faced Ruben like an old stag ready to defend his territory from the new cocky buck. "I give you more than money, Ruben. I've called in favors with a judge more than once for you and that screw up Zane, so don't be thinking I'm not fair."

"Didn't say that, Boss. Just curious."

"Good." Clay leaned back in his chair. "The barn and pay stations have already been set up. Gather some men and put them at the gates as lookouts ... just in case. I want all hands walking around and reporting anything odd. No one gets in that isn't on the guest list without my approval. All our buyers are here, and I don't give a damn about the sheriff. Obviously, only a handful of us know what is actually going on, and I want to keep it that way."

"Right." Ruben stood, and walked towards the door. He paused, then turned to face Clay.

"Yes?" Clay raised an eyebrow, sat forward and crossed his arms.

"What should I do with Mac?"

"Nothing right now. Just get the rest of the crap done, then bring her some food. Oh yeah, she's vegan."

"What the heck does that mean? No meat?"

"Means bring her peanut butter and chips."

Ruben gave a nod and left.

Clay gazed out the window. He had an unsettling feeling. Too many things going wrong. First the Keene boy, then Zane, and now Mac. Still, he had the money to dig his way out, if it all went to hell in a handbasket. Lucky for me, Texas doesn't give two cents about killing animals, he snickered to himself. As long as you fed them and kept their cages clean, you could kill as many as you wanted. Of course, throwing a woman in a cage was probably frowned upon, but Clay felt confident he had covered his bases. He'd be rid of both the horns, and Mac, soon enough.

Chapter 31:   She Went That-A-Way

Jenny stared into the dark, at the ceiling of the trailer. Though she tried, sleep eluded her. Shadows seemed to move even though Jenny knew it was just her eyes playing tricks with the lack of light. The crickets were asleep, and the quiet was deafening. Soon, she would hear the chitter-chatter of the birds waking.

"All I wanted was a house in Florida where Zane and I could start our family," she said to the ceiling, or maybe to God. "Now I feel like I'm trapped in a bad sitcom full of idiots."

Jenny looked over at the old, digital alarm clock. Five-five-nine glared at her in annoyingly red, boxy numbers. In one minute, it would be time to feed animals and do what Clay told her to do—tell Nancy that Mac had gone missing. Then what?! Mac's a grown adult. Why would Nancy even consider that anything had gone wrong, at least right away? There had to be a way to make it seem urgent.

She watched the time, determined not to move until she had to. The numbers suddenly turned into six-zero-zero. The alarm squawked, filling her with dread. Jenny sat up and let the irritating noise fill her ears.

"I'm tired of being someone's bitch," she said out loud as the alarm screamed its understanding.

Clay screwed me over. That douchebag made me an accomplice to hiding a body by getting me to give Zane the key to the lion's enclosure. Now he wants me to aid him in kidnapping and bribery. "I'm not even going to get a good cut!" She shouted at the alarm. The alarm yelled back, "*whaaa ... whaaa ... whaaa*" in outrage.

"What? Are Mac's morals a higher price than mine?" *Yes*, a voice in her mind answered. "I deserve just as much, if not more than Mac," she argued with her conscience.

No, you don't. That same, irritating, internal voice said. That voice always reminded Jenny of her mother.

"*Whaaa ... whaaa ... whaaa.*" The clock joining her in her argument with herself.

"I have worked for that man for a year. Giving him info on the rescue's financials, Keene's plans and whereabouts—all the information Clay needed to keep in his back pocket, should the need arise."

"Yet here I am. Lying on a cheap bed in a dumb trailer, talking to myself." That's when the idea hit her. Jenny got up and slammed her hand on the clock to stop its nonsense.

She quickly went into Mac's room and straight to her dresser. She opened the top drawer and moved Mac's plain black and white underwear and bras aside.

"Bingo."

Jenny picked up the folder from Keene that Mac had showed her, as well as the duplicate keys to all the enclosures. Of course, Mac hadn't hidden them. Mac trusted Jenny, and she figured no one else would ever come into the trailer. Everyone here trusted each other and never locked their doors.

Mac had told Jenny that she and Keene had spare keys to open all the exhibits. She even took her in to see that little fox one night. Now Jenny was about to break

that trust. She put the keys on top of the dresser in a
jewelry bowl that held a pair of earrings and a couple of
charm bracelets. She then took the folder and hid it in her
room, at the back of the closet. After, pleased with herself
that she had hidden the folder where no one would look,
she went back to Mac's closet.

Jenny looked for anything that resembled luggage.
She found two tattered gym bags. She grabbed as many
clothes as she could stack in her arms, then stuffed them in
the bags. She did the same with underwear and socks from
the dresser drawers. She looked around the room and
noticed some clothing had fallen to the floor. She decided
leaving whatever rogue articles that landed on the ground
alone would help set the stage for the appearance of
impatience during a hasty retreat. She took the gym bags
and shoved them deep under her bed.

With everything in place, Jenny hurriedly changed
into her dark grey cargo shorts and pulled her blue
volunteer t-shirt over her head. The initials J.A.W.S. and
her name were embroidered in bright yellow. She looked
in the mirror, leaned in, and examined the dark circles that
highlighted her bloodshot eyes.

"You look horrible," she told her reflection. Her
reflection looked backed and nodded in sync with her.
"The show must go on, but maybe not quite as Clay
planned." Her reflection gave a clever sneer.

She left her room and poured a steaming cup of
black coffee. The taste was bitter and strong. Her gut gave
a noisy squish, and she felt a slight bout of nausea as the
coffee hit her empty stomach. Jenny grabbed a Pop-Tart
from the cupboard and ate it cold. She tasted sugar,

raspberry, and dough as she swung open the squeaky aluminum door with a loud bang. She stopped in the doorway, taking in a determined breath, she headed to the rescue's prep kitchen.

It's time to do things my way.

***

The kitchen was in a large, grey, wooden barn located next to the front office. The area was used to prepare the meals for the animals. It looked like a regular chef's kitchen, minus the stove. Jenny approached a stainless-steel table and grabbed a handful of bowls of various shapes, sizes, and materials from the baker's racks on her right. All the bowls had been donated, and she liked the unconformity of them. To her left were barrels of produce donated by stores around the Kerrville, Boerne, and San Antonio areas. Large bins for compost and trash were on her right. Her job was to throw out anything rotten or non-nutritious for the animals and cut up the rest.

She picked up a large, chef's knife, grabbed a bunch of carrots, and started chopping. After the vegetables, she would chop the fruit. It was a long process, but it made a good meal for the monkeys, squirrels, bears, and rabbits. Since Mac wasn't here, what usually took an hour and left her time to goof off a bit, would now take her two hours, but she could use that time to rehearse what she was going to say to Nancy.

As Jenny sliced the last green apple, she looked up at a round, white clock that reminded her of a school clock. Eight twenty-seven, the black clock hands told her. Nancy was always in by eight-thirty. The next three minutes crawled by.

The long hand finally reached the six just as Nancy walked into the kitchen area, right on schedule for her usual check that everything was running smoothly.

"Good morning, Jenny." Nancy walked past her and visually checked out the meals she had prepared.

"Morning, Nancy." Jenny paused, putting down the chef's knife, wiping her hands with a white hand towel, and gathering her thoughts.

"Is this one for Jacob, the new black bear?" Nancy held up a large bowl with chopped vegetables, nuts, and berries. Jenny nodded.

"Don't forget the medicine. He still needs his antibiotic for another four days."

Some horrible person had kept Jacob shackled up for five years, giving him a terrible sore that still hadn't healed.

"Oh yeah, sorry. I'm not used to doing the medicine. That's usually Mac's job." Jenny reached for an envelope with the name Jacob on it in large, black Sharpie marker.

Nancy threw up her arms in a moment of frustration. "These people are so ignorant! A bear ... for a pet! I wish we could do the same to them. Let them know how it feels." Nancy turned to leave, then paused.

"Wait, where's Mac?"

"Um, I haven't seen her this morning." Jenny focused on sprinkling the powder into the food. She absently stirred it in, waiting for Nancy to say more.

"What? You mean she's still in bed? You did this all yourself? Let me help you pack it into the cart." Nancy grabbed a black grocery crate to help stack the full food bowls for transport to the hungry residents.

"No, I mean I didn't see her this morning. Her bed was made. I figured she was already feeding the animals, but I haven't seen her all morning."

Nancy stopped and looked at Jenny, then the clock.

"Did you try calling her?"

"Um, yeah, a couple of times. Goes straight to voice mail." *This isn't working,* said Jenny's annoying voice.

"Well, that is unusual for her, but she has been through a lot."

"I know. She mentioned to me yesterday that she was eager to get back to work, if only for the distraction." Jenny paused. "I'm a little worried." An empty pit of anticipation settled into her stomach.

Nancy stood up and seemed to contemplate this thought for way too long.

"Well, let's give her 'til noon. After that, maybe I'll call Sheriff Moore, unofficially. He gave me his card."

"Good idea."

Jenny didn't feel good about manipulating Nancy, but she didn't have much choice. She felt worse about what happened to Mac. Jenny had grown to care for Mac. She was hired to spy, but Clay never said she wasn't allowed to make friends, and Mac was a good friend. Jenny had lied to Mac, but she wasn't going to see her hurt or manipulated by that jackass Clay.

She'd plan to go see Zane in the hospital tomorrow. Maybe she could talk him into quitting or moving to Florida, but first she would help Mac escape.

174

Hold on 'til tonight, Mac.

Chapter 32:   I'll Take a Reuben to Go

Ruben had barked Clay's orders at the other ranch hands, then went behind the kitchen to smoke and think. The kitchen staff was busy with breakfast, so he would be free from distractions. The pleasant aroma of pancakes, bacon, and coffee wafted through the wooden screen door of the kitchen. He sat on top of one of three long, wooden, picnic tables under a pavilion at the back of the kitchen, feet resting on the bench. Every Friday the ranch threw a barbeque for the guests here, with tables full of guests, food, and beer. "It's so the rich feel like they're roughing it," Zane had commented to him once, and he was right. Half those people didn't even hunt. They sat by a feeder or in an area where the animals got cornered or trapped. Right now, though, it was nice and quiet. He was alone.

I need to bail. I have to do this smart and make sure I get what's coming to me. With a metal click of a lid hinge, the dry sound of the flint wheel turning, and the sizzle of burning paper, he lit a Winston cigarette with a plain, steel Zippo. It had been his dad's and was probably as old as he was. He watched a stream of smoke leave his lungs in a long exhale. The heat burned his throat in a comforting way. The sun still gave a pink glow to the morning sky as he sat there, lost in his thoughts.

I'm doing all the work, and Mac is going to get more money than me. Ruben looked down at his weathered hands and examined them. I'm not going to leave empty-handed. I can get cash tonight. In the morning, Clay will miss me, but he'll be too busy with the auction to act. He took another deep drag from the

Winston as he watched the horses eating grass in the pasture. It would soon be time to saddle them up for a trail ride. He'd have to move quickly.

I know there is a safe in the office; the same building where Mac is, and I know Clay keeps money in there most of the time. He uses it to stash the under-the-table money and sometimes his winnings in the high-stakes poker games he throws over there. I also know the combo; Clay's mom's birthday, Ruben chuckled to himself. Clay had given Ruben the combo a long time ago during a drunken poker game, hopefully he hadn't changed it.

I'll go give Mac her food and water, then check on the stash and make sure there is enough to make it worth my while to bolt right now. If not, there will be plenty of time after the auction, but I'd rather not stick around to see if Mac takes the bribe. She's stubborn and smart. Hell, what's to stop her from taking the bribe and running to the sheriff anyway?

These shady deals of Clay's are catching up to him. First, he started illegally importing exotics for captive breeding and caged hunts, then the auctions. Now, I'm moving bodies and kidnapping women. It's getting harder to justify the pay. The stakes keep getting bigger, and so do the jail time sentences. What's it going to be next? I couldn't give a lick about the animals. The auction doesn't worry me either, but Mac does.

He took another big inhale of the cigarette, holding the hot smoke in his lungs, then watching it dance in front of his face as he steadily exhaled through his nose. Mac is a loose cannon, and I'm not going to jail ... for anyone. He thought about Zane. He shouldn't feel guilty leaving him behind; he didn't really owe him anything. Ruben didn't miss the irony of leaving Zane alone, the same way his father did, though. *I'll come back. After things die down, I will come back for him. Or maybe I will pick him up on the way. Hopefully, Jenny wouldn't be there, and they could leave town without her.*

Ruben went to the kitchen pantry and pulled out peanut butter, chips, cookies, an apple, and grabbed two cokes from the refrigerator. Once he was loaded up, he headed for the captives: Tony the tiger, whose life was going to end tomorrow in a hunt; and Mac, that saucy, crazy, hot, pain in the butt of an activist. He assumed he'd get some peace and quiet when Keene died, but Mac had taken up where he left off.

Chapter 33:   Do Not Feed the Animals

Ruben stepped from his truck. He decided to park around the back as to avoid drawing any attention, should someone drive by the building. The air was still, warm, and smelled of animals. It reminded him of going to the zoo when he was little.

He had expected to hear Mac screaming for help as he walked around the building, but he heard nothing except the chattering of birds. He immediately began to worry. What if she had escaped? Ruben quickly dismissed that thought, knowing that there was no way out of her cage. The few windows in there were really high up and too small for a person to get through. He keyed in the code, opened the door, and walked in. The automatic lights came on, but there was enough light from the small windows that it didn't make much of a difference. He heard the animals move, but none made any noises. It was eerie.

"Who's there?" Ruben heard Mac ask. He didn't answer. She would know soon enough. He walked up to the cage as Mac walked to the bars between them.

"You can't keep me here." Her hair was greasy, and she looked tired and mad.

"I'm not keeping you here. Clay is." That was the truth.

"Why don't you let me go, and I won't tell the police you were involved." Ruben had to admit that suggestion definitely tempted him.

"Here." Ruben handed Mac the bag with the food and drinks through the bars. Mac grabbed it and looked inside.

"Seriously?! You're keeping me here? Are you stupid?!"

"Screw you. You're the one who decided to go all Nancy Drew and pull your super sleuth bull hockey."

"Yeah, well I guess finding your boyfriend dead makes you kind of suspicious."

Mac stared into Ruben's eyes. Ruben stared back at Mac's blue eyes swimming in a sea of sleepless red. He was turned on and off at the same time.

"Just drink your Cokes and eat … or starve to death. I don't care." Ruben walked away to the front office.

"When did you become an evil douchebag?" Mac yelled at him, followed by the hiss of the Coke can being opened. She was probably pretty thirsty by now, Ruben thought, but she'll live. And from what Clay said, she'll be living pretty well, soon enough.

Ruben grabbed the handle to open the office door when he heard a vehicle pull up. He stopped and stepped back from the office.

"Hey! Can anyone hear me?" Mac began to yell. Ruben ran back to her cage.

"Shut up!"

"Or what?" Mac took in a deep breath and looked about to exhale with a yell. Ruben pulled out his .44 Magnum and pointed it at her face. Mac's breath quietly deflated.

"You think that's going to stop me?"

"No." Ruben slowly swung the barrel until its aim rested between Tony's eyes. "But you yell, and Tony dies right now." Ruben kept his voice low and angry. He saw the fight fade from her eyes. "Clay is going to let you go after the auction, so if you don't want to see this tiger's brains all over the goddamn cell, I suggest you shut the hell up and crawl back under that blanket." Ruben could see hate in Mac's stare. Tears filled her eyes, then she quickly turned her head and slowly stepped away from the bars, moving back towards the blanket.

Ruben walked quickly and quietly toward the door and listened. He heard six short beeps as the buttons for the code were pushed, then one long beep. Someone was at the keypad, entering the code wrong. Again—six short beeps, followed by a long beep. This time Ruben heard cursing, but he couldn't make out the words. Six beeps again. More cussing. There was a small window in the office. If he could make it there, he might be able to see who was trying to enter. He had left the office door partially open. He was bigger than the opening, but if he moved the door slowly ...

A loud creak of the hinge provoked a roar from Tony, and the other animals began to bleat and yell in their own native tongues.

Ruben heard the stranger at the door run. He also hurried to the door and cracked it open. A black SUV spit rocks and fishtailed from side to side, covering itself in a dust cloud as it hurried away along the path. Ruben choked on the dust and ran back to his truck. He wasn't going to follow too quickly. He just had to look for the SUV with dust on it to know who was here and maybe figure out why. It was probably one of the bidders looking for the horns or just being nosey.

Ruben jumped in his truck and left Mac. He didn't get a chance to check the safe, but he would do that tonight. If it has money, I bolt. If it doesn't, I'll stay until after the auction.

Chapter 34:   Have You Seen My Keys?

Jenny drove from one habitat to the next, dropping off food. Some of the animals, like the bears, donkeys, and owls, she liked. Others just creeped the hell out of her. She found monkeys unsettling ever since her dad made her watch that old *Planet of the Apes* movie when she was five. Julius really frightened her. She even refused to see the remake with Zane. Because Mac knew how Jenny felt about the monkeys, Mac usually fed them for her. Poor Mac, Jenny thought. She really didn't deserve this.

An hour later, Jenny returned to the barn and parked the cart under a huge elm tree to keep the leather from getting hot. She noticed Nancy walking over to her trailer. Jenny followed and caught up to her as she was knocking on the door.

"Oh good, Jenny! I'm glad you're here." Nancy waved for her to join her.

"I just wanted to see if Mac was back. Mind if I go in?" Nancy could have walked in, but she was always proper and polite.

"Oh, of course not."

"Thank you, Jenny. I'm a little concerned. I hope she is back."

"Me too!" Jenny slid past Nancy and opened the trailer door. Nancy walked in and stood in the family/dining area, not going in further.

"Mac? It's Nancy. Are you home?" Silence and the sound of wind on the metal trailer were all they heard.

"Which one is Mac's bedroom, again?" she asked. Jenny pointed down the small hall. "Mac's is the first one on the left, mine's on the right." Jenny led the way, with Nancy close behind. When they got to Mac's door, Jenny gave a soft knock and waited, even though she knew no one was going to answer.

"Mac? Hey, if you are in there, I'm opening the door." Jenny slipped a bladed hand through the door, trying to act cautious, as if Mac might be changing her clothes. She called out one more time as she opened the door fully, then stepped forward and off to the side so Nancy could walk in.

"The bed hasn't been slept in. That's how I found it this morning," Jenny said. Jenny looked at Nancy and saw her eye the random clothing and open closet in the room.

"This looks like she might have gone somewhere." Nancy glanced around the room. "Did she say anything to you about visiting family?"

"No, nothing ... which isn't like her," Jenny feigned concern.

Nancy walked over to the closet but didn't move things or try to look around. "Seems like clothes are missing. Bed is made. This is unusual." She walked towards the dresser. Jenny was afraid that Nancy would miss it, but she didn't.

"Wait." Nancy said and grabbed the keys from the bowl. "No."

"What?" Jenny forced a curious expression.

"This is a copy of all the keys to the exhibits." Nancy turned to Jenny and held the keys up accusingly. "Did you know about these?" The keys jangled at Jenny.

"Um, what do you mean?"

"This is a copy of the enclosure keys. There should be *no* copies of the enclosure keys! There should be a set to check out every morning, and I have one other copy." Nancy stared at the keys angrily, as if it was their fault they were in the bowl.

"Is it a big deal? I mean, it's Mac. She's really good with the animals." I set this up perfect, Jenny thought.

"Yes, it's a big deal!" Nancy yelled back. "Look!" She held up one key in particular. Jenny gave her a confused look. She could feel the hairs on the back of her neck rise, in fear of getting caught.

"It's the lion enclosure key!" Nancy's face was in a panic. She stared at Jenny. "Jenny, this suggests Mac had access to the enclosure Keene was found in."

"What are you saying?" Jenny tried to lead Nancy to her own conclusion.

"I'm saying we need to call the sheriff." Nancy took her cell phone and Sheriff Moore's card from her pocket and began to dial. As Nancy looked down at the card, Jenny caught a glimpse of her own reflection. She was smiling.

Chapter 35:   Lost and Found

This wasn't what Jenny had in mind at all. She was sitting in Nancy's office staring at Nancy behind her desk. Sheriff Moore stood beside her, looking down at Jenny.

Nancy sat with her back straight up, looking like an overreacting teacher who just caught the kid who put a tack on her chair. She was twisting a tissue in her hands. The sheriff looked cold and unyielding. He had the look of those traffic cops that act like they listen to what you say but hand you a ticket anyway. Every time he shifted his weight, the wooden floor boards creaked in protest.

Jenny could smell cat food from the four bowls that fed the feline occupants of the offices. She could see one cat, Jester. He was a long-haired calico and the friendliest of the quartet. Jasper, Titi, and Mo-mo were probably hiding in their boxes, waiting for the big strange human with the attitude and the gun to leave.

"Were Mac and Keene getting along?" The sheriff looked at Jenny.

"Of course! I mean, most of the time," Jenny answered, involuntarily sitting up straighter.

Nancy gave Jenny a quizzical look, and Jenny continued.

"They had a little spat about a week ago, but it was nothing. I mean, it's nothing now. They made up."

"What was it about?" Sheriff Moore stepped closer to Jenny, which made her uncomfortable.

She didn't like that. Can he smell that I'm lying? Can he see I'm sweating? Nancy seemed to lean in toward her too. Jenny didn't know if that meant she was curious or if she could see through her façade.

"Mac thought Keene was sleeping with someone else, but Keene said he wasn't." *Liar*, the inner voice was back. She always hated that inner voice.

"Why didn't you tell that to Sheriff Moore the other day?!" Nancy's voice was high and accusatory.

"It didn't seem important. It's Mac, for god's sake! She wouldn't hurt a fly, let alone Keene. Besides, they patched it up!"

"Still would have been good information to know," the sheriff said. "I understand you want to be a good friend, but some people do crazy things for money and love."

Jenny understood the money and love part. She'd do anything for Zane.

"Did you see or hear her packing her things?"

"No ... I ... um ... no." Jenny started to feel like maybe she hadn't thought this through very well. She just wanted this interrogation to end.

"And you knew about the spare keys."

"What? No! I never said that?" Jenny looked at Nancy questioningly. Nancy was still holding the keys she found in the bedroom and softly turning each key, one at a time, around the loop in a nervous cycle.

"But Nancy noticed you weren't that disturbed when she mentioned the keys."

"Why should I be? We all work here, and Mac is like a supervisor. She's one of the best with the lions."

"Who would be the other?" the sheriff questioned.

"Other what?"

"Other 'best lion person'."

"Keene," Nancy interjected. "Keene was very good with the lions."

"Yet, he was attacked." The sheriff took a moment before continuing. "I'm going to have my deputies look for her." Sheriff Moore put a hand on Nancy's shoulder. "Don't worry, I'm sure it's nothing, but I believe we need to find her." Jenny relaxed. She had gotten the response she needed from Nancy and the sheriff. As she contemplated on what she needed to do to prepare for tonight, thunder rumbled in the distance.

Chapter 36:   Oh Where, Oh Where, has My Activist Went?

The mug felt hot in his hand, and the coffee smelled bitter and strong. He stood, leaning up against the counter, absently blowing the steam. Sheriff Moore drank from his stained cup. He never washed it, claiming it added to the flavor. He didn't think anyone cleaned the coffee pot for the same reason. He could hear the thunder outside.

"Frickin rain," he mumbled under his breath.

Deputy Allen walked into the breakroom and poured himself a cup. He added a large amount of half-and-half and three spoonfuls of sugar.

"You want some coffee with that cream and sugar, Chris?"

"The coffee here is awful. I can't believe you drink it black."

"I've had worse," Sheriff Moore replied, although he couldn't recall when.

"Really? Were you in prison?" They both chuckled at this.

"The coffee is actually good there." Sheriff Moore noticed the confused look on the Deputy's face. "I was a warden for a year. Job was the worst, but the coffee was good."

"And now you are in a quiet Texas town, just like in the movies, and the coffee sucks." The deputy inspected a box of donuts left from the morning.

"I wouldn't say it's quiet right now." The sheriff walked over to the donuts. "Got any powdered in there?"

"Yep, right there." The deputy pointed. "Well, half a donut anyway. If you're going to eat a donut, just commit and take the whole thing. People are so health paranoid now."

"It's probably best I have the half." Sheriff Moore patted the beginnings of a small pooch. "Age is starting to go up, metabolism is starting to go down." He grimaced at the donut but took a bite anyway.

"Thinking about the Keene boy?"

"It just doesn't make sense." Sheriff More leaned over the box as he bit into the donut, so the sugar would drop back into the box." The deputy gave him a disgusted look.

"What?" The sheriff mumbled with his mouth full.

"How about a napkin instead of sprinkling your donut spit on everything," the deputy said as he picked up a powder-free chocolate donut. "What in particular bothers you? The "Was it a cougar," or "Was it an African lion," or the question of how he got in the enclosure?" The deputy sat at the break table as he bit into his donut. "Or why is Mac all of a sudden missing? Obviously, she took off, taking the missing clothes and car into consideration."

A loud clasp of thunder caused them both to pause and the sound of rain started at full force, skipping the politeness of a warning sprinkle.

"That's just what we need. More rain," the deputy stated tiresomely.

"Well, we know Keene was moved," the sheriff started. "But why move him? At first, I presumed Clay might have something to do with this, but then Mac leaves without a word to her employer or her best friend. She has

190

keys to the lion's enclosure, but she also tried to show me a folder Keene gave her. It contained information he learned from all his spying and protesting at the ranch." The sheriff paused to take another bite of his donut. This time he held his hand underneath. He took a sip of the still scalding coffee to wash the donut down. "I don't have enough evidence to go search Clay's ranch, and I really don't want to piss Clay off for nothing. Don't get me wrong. I don't mind pissing him off, I just want a legitimate reason."

"What about Zane? Did he say anything?"

"Nah, but I'm going to go back there tomorrow morning. I'm pretty sure I can get something out of him. In the meantime, I have a BOLO out on Mac's car, so hopefully she will turn up soon, and we can get some answers."

The thunder had stopped, but the rain still poured, sounding as if the building was located under a waterfall.

"She may have just gone to see family," Deputy Allen commented. "I mean, she wasn't an actual suspect, and she's an adult. Not much we can do, *legally,* at least for another day."

"I know." Sheriff Moore headed for his office. "But why leave without telling anyone?" His gut was telling him there was more. "Of course, the main suspect is missing."

"Who is that?"

"The cougar," the sheriff replied. "Where the hell is the cougar?"

"Jenny mentioned Mac and Keene had a fight. That Mac thought Keene was sleeping around. Think that is enough motive?"

"Love and jealousy can always be motives, but I didn't get that feeling from Mac when I talked with her. Are you suggesting murder?"

"Ha! That would be scandal!" The deputy shoved that last half of donut in his mouth.

"Scandal or not, it's not impossible ... but I think it's unlikely. I'll see Zane in the morning. I'm sure I can get some answers."

"Good luck with that one," the deputy stood. "Let me know if you want me to come. I could use the entertainment."

"I think I'll head over to Clay's." Sheriff Moore stated. The deputy was about to speak when they were interrupted by a fellow officer's head peeking into the breakroom.

"Sir, the river's spilled its banks. One high water rescue already, two more called in. It came in fast. The weather is starting to let up, but it looks like the next few hours are going to jammed packed with fun."

"Crap." Deputy Allen said flatly. "Looks like Clay gets a reprieve from Mother Nature."

Sheriff Moore sighed as he quickly left to retrieve his rain gear.

"I'll go see him tomorrow, after I talk with Zane."

192

Chapter 37:   You Did It

It seemed like she listened to falling rain for most of the night. Thunder made Tony nervous. He would pace after every rumble. Mac was glad when the it had faded and finally stopped. That seemed to settle him, so she could sleep. She didn't know what time it was, but knew it was the early morning hours. Maybe three? Maybe four? She made a mental note to go back to wearing watches. She could see how silly it was that she relied on her phone to tell her the time.

The lock to the front door beeped. She could hear it open and someone wiping their feet on a mat. Mac stood up quickly, and Tony launched himself at the cage wall standing between him and Mac. Mac yelled as she fell over. A large paw reached through the space, between the bars, and clawed at the air between them. Tony's head was pressed firmly against the cage, his hot, dark-smelling breath reaching Mac's nose. She was frightened, but she also felt empathy for him. He was put in this strange place solely for the entertainment of humans and had every right to be angry.

Mac went over to the cage door and looked down the hallway to see who had come in. The hall lights automatically came on, and Mac saw a figure looking back towards the door, appearing to look outside. The figure wiped their feet on the mat again, then turned.

"Oh my God! Jenny! Help! Over here!" Mac waved through the bars at Jenny.

"Mac, you're all right ... thank goodness!" Jenny exclaimed, jogging down the hallway. Her boots squeaked with each step and small drops of mud randomly fell from the tops. When the two women were face to face, they simultaneously grasp hands from between the bars, as if one of them would disappear if they let go. Aside from the boots, Mac noticed Jenny was bone dry.

"How did you know I was here?"

"It's a long story, Mac. Let's just find a way to get you out." Jenny's eyes focused on Tony, and she jumped back. "Oh my god! They put you next to that!" Tony licked his lips in response.

"He's just another victim in all this. They are going to kill him tomorrow. I can't let that happen."

"I'm not real sure how you think you can stop them, Mac."

"I haven't figured that out yet, but Clay is selling rhino horns. That's what Keene was trying to figure out, or get proof of, or whatever … before he died! Those are worth hundreds of thousands, Jenny. Clay is supporting the poaching of endangered animals! I saw them—twelve black rhino horns, Jenny! … Twelve!"

"What do you mean rhino horns?"

Mac started to pace and wave her arms in anger. Jenny and Tony watched as Mac pontificated.

"Twelve dead rhinos, just so some businessman with an ego, or an erection issue, or the promise from a witch doctor that it cures cancer, can feel better about himself. God, people sicken me! It's made of frickin' fingernail, Jenny! FRICKIN' FINGERNAIL!"

Tony stood and started pacing frantically, as if Mac's speech had angered him as well.

"Mac! Calm down, let's focus on getting you back to the trailer." Before Mac could say anymore, Jenny ran off to the office by the front door. Mac could hear the opening and closing of wooden drawers. After what seemed like a lifetime, Jenny came running out with a handful of keys.

"Let's hope one of these works."

Mac held onto the bars like prisoners did in the movies, as Jenny tried the keys. The third key hit home with a click. Mac pushed the door open and embraced Jenny.

"Thank you, thank you, and thank you." Mac felt like, if this *were* a movie, it should be a crying moment, but she didn't feel like crying. She felt like kicking ass.

She held Jenny at arm's length. "Let's get to a phone and call the sheriff."

"Mac, let's get out of here first. I have my car by a back entrance, but it's a little bit of a walk. We need to get out of here. Let's just forget about this, and maybe they'll leave us alone."

Mac blinked at Jenny like she was speaking a foreign language.

"What are you talking about, Jenny? Clay is selling illegal rhino horns. Keene is dead because of this somehow, and we have to find a way to save Tony!"

"OH, MY GOD, JUST STOP!" Jenny yelled. Mac stepped back, stunned by the harshness of her outburst.

"Let's just forget about all this!" Jenny gestured all around her. "Let's just get back to life. Save some frickin' deer back at the rescue and just go back to simple stuff. No "save the world" agenda! No rhino horns! Just simple work, eat, drink, screw, and sleep."

Mac couldn't believe what she was hearing. Jenny wasn't talking like someone who was serious about animal lives. Mac had always doubted Jenny's level of commitment since she first met her two years ago. She was hired shortly after the sheriff had a talk with Keene about not trespassing on Big Bear Ranch. A dawning expression came across Mac's face.

"Jenny. How did you know I was here?"

Tears started to well in Jenny's eyes. "It ... it ... was Zane who told me. We've been dating for a year." Mac was horrified.

"He's not that bad, Mac! Really. He's a little misguided, but he's a good guy. He works; he tries hard."

"So, you've been dating Zane and working at the rescue. How does that fit together, Jenny? Why didn't you mention this? Are you spying on the rescue, or what?"

Jenny hung her head for a moment, then looked straight at Mac. "Yes, a little. Well, mostly on Keene. I needed a job, and Zane asked me if I could work at the rescue. Clay gives Zane extra money for it." Mac felt fire in her eyes and narrowed her gaze on Jenny. She could see that Jenny saw her anger, as Jenny stepped back in fear.

"Mac, they just wanted to know what Keene was doing because he kept trespassing. It didn't seem like a big deal, and I didn't know about the horns, so it only seemed like Keene was breaking the law. I would just let them know when he left or if I saw anything ... but I really didn't have that much info to give, and I didn't expect us to become really good friends. By the time we were, I didn't know how to tell you."

"So ... what about Keene's death, Jenny? How did he end up in the cage with Xena and Thor?"

"I had no idea what they were doing that night, I swear to you!" Mac grabbed Jenny by the arms and yelled, "What did they do to Keene!" Tony roared in response, making them both jump.

"That night, almost morning, Zane just came and asked about the keys to the cage. When you found Keene, I was just as shocked as you! I asked Zane about it later, and he told me they found Keene in one of their enclosures. That Keene was sneaking around and got attacked, and that they couldn't let the death hurt Clay's business, so they moved him. No one killed him, Mac! He got killed because he snuck onto Clay's property! It was his own fault!"

Mac slapped Jenny, which surprised them both. Her hand stung from the slap, and Jenny held her face, as tears started to roll down her reddening cheek.

"I'm so sorry." Jenny's voice was a raspy whisper. "I didn't want any of this to happen, and things got out of hand so quickly. I really am sorry. I want to fix this, Mac. I just don't want to go to jail ... I didn't mean for any of this to happen."

Mac knew Jenny was telling the truth. She was still mad, but she also saw Jenny as very naïve, just another pawn in Clay's game.

"Look, I'm furious at you, but I believe you." Mac put her hands on her hips. "But now you know, and it's too late to just sit back and do nothing. You have to do what is right. You've been manipulated, whether you want to admit it or not, but you did come and let me out, so that means something." A look of relief washed over Jenny's face.

"Okay, we need to figure this out," Mac continued. "We need to get Sheriff Moore here without tipping off Clay. We also need to save Tony. It's almost morning now. You're going to save him, and I'm going to stop the auction."

Jenny wiped her tears and looked at Tony, who had taken perch on a wooden pallet; intently watching the exchange, then back at Mac.

"Okay. I'm in. But how the hell am I going to do that?"

"I'm going to get the sheriff. You stay here and stall anyone who comes. Since you're dating Zane, they won't shove you in a cage." Mac could see this comment stung Jenny, but she didn't feel too guilty about it after having to pee in a bucket.

Mac saw Jenny look at Tony. Tony stared at Jenny as if to say, "Yeah, and you'd better do it."

"I'm not going to stand in front of a gun for it." Jenny looked at Mac with pleading eyes. "I was planning on setting you free, then going to see Zane."

"You don't get it." Mac was disappointed in Jenny, but she was more disappointed in herself for thinking Jenny understood animals and understood her. "We are all victims. Tony's life was exploited. He deserves to live as much as we do."

"He isn't going to believe you." Jenny replied flatly. "The sheriff, I mean."

"Why wouldn't he?" Mac remembered Sheriff Moore's question about her whereabouts when Keene died.

"Nancy was concerned when you didn't show up for work. So was I. She looked in your drawer and found the keys and called Sheriff Moore. She said this implied you had access to the lion cage and that she had to tell the sheriff and let him do the investigating. It looks bad for you, Mac."

"Why were they in my room? Wait a minute. When did you know I was here?" Mac felt anger rising inside her again. Jenny held her hands up as if in defense, palms up.

"I didn't know you were here till like an few hours ago. The rain held me up. I had to wait until the roads were clear."

Mac didn't know whether she believed her, but at this point, she wasn't sure that mattered right now.

"Dammit." Mac thought for a moment. "Then I will just have to pick up some proof on the way.

"What does that mean?"

"I'll get one of the horns. Where is the auction being held, Jenny?"

"I don't know about an auction, but I would assume it would be in the building that looks like a school or a church. I think it was used as both decades ago, but Mac, please, let's just both leave."

"Look, you owe me! You owe Keene!" The anger was back. "If you would have told Nancy or the sheriff what Clay was doing, maybe Keene wouldn't be dead!" Mac saw tears flow down Jenny's face. "Look, just stay here. If the sheriff or I am not back in two hours ... leave."

Mac dropped to a soft tone. "I know this sounds stupid, and it won't bring Keene back, but I feel like if I can at least save this beautiful animal, or can get Clay charged with selling the rhino horns, then Keene didn't die for nothing." Jenny seemed to take a moment to mull over Mac's words.

"Okay. I'll stay."

"Thank you!" Mac hugged Jenny, not giving her time to return the hug before heading for the door.

"Mac!" Jenny yelled at her. Mac stopped and turned. Jenny fished in her pocket and brought out a set of car keys. She tossed them at Mac, who easily caught them.

"Follow the road at the back of this building. It will lead you all the way to the old school house and the main grounds. It's going to take you about twenty minutes or more before you see it. If you walk on the thick weeds, you can manage to stay out of the mud ... anyway, stay close to the fence where they won't see you. Once you're almost behind the schoolhouse, you should see a break in the fence, that's where my car is."

"Thanks." Mac said. Mac turned to leave, paused, then looked back at Jenny. "Thanks, for coming for me. I'm still mad, but I also know you did me a solid by coming back for me."

"Yeah." Jenny looked at her feet, then back up at Mac. "Just hurry. This tiger gives me the chills."

Mac turned and ran out.

***

Jenny stood still a long time after watching Mac leave. She had no intention of staying here for more than ten or fifteen minutes. She lied to Mac about how Nancy found the keys, and she left out the big lie about hiding her clothes, but all that didn't matter now. She rescued Mac,

200

and now she could go see Zane. She just needed to give Mac a head start—

Suddenly blackness surrounded her. Her heart jumped, then started to beat rapidly. I can't see! Why can't I see?! The voice in Jenny's head gave a scream, but Jenny couldn't move, and fear grasped her voice. The initial panic began to subside as she remembered the motion detectors. Shadows formed as her eyes adjusted to the darkness. Still finding herself paralyzed, she listened. She could hear her own heart beating, slowly. Another sound crept in ... a deep, rhythmic breath.

That's just Tony. Don't be stupid, Jenny. The tiger is in his cage.

She pictured the giant cat somehow vaporizing and appearing at her side. Her mind had not only gotten the best of her but was taking her on a wild ride. Jenny could feel her knees getting weak and her head dizzy. Her immobility and panic attack were broken by the sound of a vehicle approaching. She moved, and the lights came on.

Jenny let out a squeak and did a comical step to the right, saw Tony, stumbled back to the left, saw a wall, then focused on the janitor's closet. She stopped.

"Get it together!" she whispered to herself. Whoever is coming, is expecting Mac to be in that cage.

Jenny remembered she still had the keys. Looking in the cage, she noticed the blanket. Thinking quickly, she got in, flinching at the sound of locking herself in a cell next to a tiger. She bundled up in the musty blanket.

"Eww, gross." Animal and piss. I am literally wrapping myself in animal piss. I am so done with all this.

She scooted close into the far corner of the wall and hoped
to fool whoever was coming. She didn't have a better plan.

Chapter 38:   Grrrreat!

As Ruben pulled up to the animal holding building, the lights inside turned on. Probably a mouse. He had an unnerving image that he would go in and find both Mac and the money gone. It's bad enough I had to wait for the rain to stop, he complained to himself, now I'm being paranoid. Keep it together, just a few hours off schedule. If anything, this is better. Clay will be too busy with the auction to look for me.

Ruben quickly got out of the truck but left it running for a speedy exit. Once I get the money, I need to get the hell out of here.

Ruben reflexively slipped his hand under his black jacket. Like teenagers searching for their smart phone, a sense of calm flowed through him at the touch of his .44, securely holstered underneath. He grabbed a large, empty, black canvas backpack and jogged inside.

He had to ensure that Mac was in her cell first. Animals rustled as he walked down the hall. Something seemed off, but he couldn't put a finger on it. There were bits of dirt on the floor, but he couldn't be sure he hadn't left those. He walked up to the cell and saw the small female shape in the corner, her head covered by a dirty blanket, concealing her face. For a moment he felt sorry for Mac, but then reminded himself that she was about to get a lot of money for just sleeping on the floor for a night or two.

"Good. You're still here."

"Umph." The swaddled figure replied and repositioned herself closer to the wall.

"Well, you'll be happy to know I'm quitting, as of right now. Enjoy the rest of your night." Ruben turned back for the office and talked loudly. "By the way, your cell mate is getting a canned hunt tomorrow. They're just going to lead him to the outside cage, and Mr. Lui is going to shoot him. Apparently, tiger balls give you longer erections. I doubt it, but why the hell should I care? Probably a lot simpler to take a blue pill, but whatever floats their boat."

Ruben turned and strolled to the office. He marveled at his savior, the antique 1950's black Smith & Davis four-hundred-pound safe. It had ornate artwork on it, with an emblem of an eagle. Ruben leaned down and looked and the numbers on the dial.

Please let the combo be the same, he hoped. He rubbed his hands together and breathed into them as if to warm them on a cold day. He gave his knuckles and audible *crack,* then spun the dial right to the number ten. Then cautiously spun it left, passing the number nineteen once and settling on it the second time. He felt his brow begin to perspire. He turned the dial right, slowly to the number forty-seven. He heard a familiar click, turned the lever with a loud *clunk*, and smiled as he opened the heavy door.

"Jackpot!" he yelled and laughed to the room. There were bounded stacks of hundred-dollar bills.

"Hah! There has to be over a half a million in here. You hear that, Red? Too bad I don't like redheads. Could have taken you with me." He received no response from Mac.

"What? You actually have nothing to say?" Ruben felt the cash was appropriate payback for all the hell he had just been through. He started filling the backpack when he heard a screeching noise. That can't be a cage door he told himself. He put the money and the pack down slowly, then stepped out of the office.

"What the fu–?" There stood Mac … standing outside the cage. But the figure was too short to be Mac. No! Definitely not Mac!

"How the hell did you get here, Jenny? What the hell! What are you doing here?" Ruben started walking quickly towards her.

"Did you let Mac out? You stupid woman! You have really screwed things up!" Ruben could feel the veins in his forehead pulse as his anger imploded. Zane's girlfriend or not, Jenny had ticked him off and she had her hand on the tiger's cage.

"Stop right there!" Jenny yelled and shoved the key into the cage lock.

"What the hell?"

"You need to give me and Zane half of that money!" Jenny demanded.

"Are you crazy?" He couldn't believe what he was hearing. Ruben looked at the tiger. He was dangerously close to the door, ears back, muscles tightened to a spring-like tension. Ruben contemplated if he could make it to Jenny in time to break her fingers.

"I want out of here too. Me and Zane deserve to get out of this hole of a town."

"Do you think you can intimidate me!" Ruben stepped forward and heard the click of the key.

"Don't come any closer! I will open this door!"

"You're not that stupid." As the words left Ruben's mouth, Jenny pulled back, leaving a sliver of a gap between the door and its latch.

Ruben saw the next few seconds in slow motion and fast forward at the same time. The tiger leapt forward towards the cage door. Jenny caught the movement and pushed the door shut in reaction, while Ruben reached for his forty-four. As Ruben pulled the gun from its holster, the door shot open with the weight of the tiger, slamming Jenny up against the bars, and the edge of the door hitting his hand and knocking the gun to the floor.

Ruben was now staring directly into the tiger's gold eyes, his empty gun hand still raised. The tiger seemed to be assessing his new situation. Ruben didn't have long to react. He glanced down at his forty-four.

If I dive down, I can make it, roll right, then shoot him. Ruben looked back at the tiger. No one was moving. Jenny was holding the door close to her, eyes wide with panic. A lifetime seemed to go by while Ruben waited for his chance ... or was it a couple of minutes?

The lights in the room suddenly went black. Ruben dove towards the direction he last saw the gun. He caught the glimpse of a dark shadow from the corner of his eye before he felt a crushing weight push him to the ground.

He screamed once, then couldn't scream again.

Chapter 39:   Watch Your Step

Jenny was dazed, but the horrible scream snapped her back to the present danger. The motion of the attack turned the lights back on as she witnessed the horrid sight of Ruben, with Tony's mouth around his neck. Jenny saw him scratching and clawing for his life, the gun right under his feet. Jenny knew there's no way for her to reach the gun without getting herself killed.

Tony's low, baritone growl seemed to confirm her thoughts as it melded with Ruben's gurgling sounds, making a morbid ballad as the blood poured from his mouth and neck. Jenny couldn't take her eyes from the thick red blood, now pooling at his feet and creeping towards her. Ruben started to punch Tony's head, but his hits were quickly reduced to mere love taps, as the strength left his body.

Jenny got up slowly and slid herself to the wall, following it like a lifeline. She tried not to look at the gruesome sight of man versus tiger but couldn't stop herself. Ruben's hits had stopped. Jenny looked at Ruben's face. She saw his eyes focus on her—pleading, terrified. He appeared to be trying to say something to her, but nothing came out but the blood dripping from his lips. He raised a hand to her, as if she could pull him away. Jenny then saw the life fade from his eyes, almost immediately turning cloudy and empty, as his arm dropped, and his body went slack.

Tony slowly let go of Ruben's neck, and he slid with a wet smack onto the blood-soaked floor. He lay down beside Ruben and started to lick the blood slowly pumping from his neck, like a mother cat cleaning her kitten. If I get out of this mess, I will never forget that sound.

She started to move, but her foot slipped in the blood, barely hitting Tony, but startling him and distracting him from his prey. He looked up and stared at Jenny, as if contemplating a second dinner. She scooted along the floor, smearing Ruben's blood in a morbid trail on the concrete, as she pulled herself to the office.

"Nice kitty ... kitty," Jenny whispered in a breathless plea, her hands using the wall as a guide.

Tony stood and began slowly walking towards her. With each foot Jenny got nearer to the door, Tony got closer to her. Please don't let me die.

Jenny felt a space behind her as she reached the open office door. She rolled in, got quickly to her knees, and grasped the side of the door. As she closed it, she could see Tony quickly cover the last few feet in one bound. Gold and black filled the small space as the door clicked shut, and she turned the lock.

She could hear Tony inhale deeply, nose to the crack at the bottom of the door. Sounds like someone snorting coke. The noise invoked a random memory. A crazy night about two years ago, when she and three of her friends left a bar with two rich guys. She thought the private party would be cool. Instead, they all ended up watching some douche snort coke and talk about his boat, while the other got sloppy drunk and tried to get in her pants. She faked a migraine, and they all left, leaving the two boys to play with each other if they wanted; she didn't care.

Large claws scratched at the door, sounding more curious than vicious. Jenny crab-walked backward toward the wall. When she felt something strange touch her hand, she almost screamed.

Turning around, she saw an open backpack. Relief washed over her. Jenny's eyes widened as she saw what was in the bag ... money ... lots of it. Her eyes followed the money to the open safe. The scratching at the door had stopped. Jenny assumed Tony had gone back to Ruben.

"Holy—not possible," she whispered to herself. So, this is what that bastard was up to ... no, it didn't feel right thinking of him that way now ... now that he was dead. "Zane, baby, we are leaving town."

Jenny scrambled to her feet and started to shove as much money in the bag as the zipper allowed. She picked up the backpack, testing the weight. Heavy, but I got this.

She got up quietly and looked around the office, searching for an exit. She considered the window. She quickly deduced it was too small, even for her tiny frame. Jenny looked out the window. It was almost black with dirt, but she could make out the truck and see puffs from the hot exhaust touching the cool night, reflecting in the building's front lights.

"Thank you, Ruben, for keeping the truck running." Jenny turned to the door. It was the only way out.

She would need to run while Tony was preoccupied. It wasn't far from the office door to the front door, but it seemed like miles with a hungry tiger loose in the room. Jenny took a deep breath, adjusted the heavy backpack on her shoulders, and headed for the door.

She slowly turned the handle and carefully opened the door, just enough to look into the hall. Tony was lying down close to Ruben. Jenny thought if someone were to walk in now, they would think the two were cuddling, and Tony was giving Ruben tender licks.

Jenny inched her way out. She felt numb and a little dizzy, a tingling sensation rising from her feet as she walked backwards, ready to sprint if Tony spotted her.

Jenny froze for a second as she looked and noticed Tony's licks had turned to pulls on Ruben's skin ... and he was watching her from his peripheral vision. The dizziness and tingling sensation grew stronger. She had fainted before, and she knew this feeling was the start of it.

No, Jenny! Keep it together. Thoughts of being attacked by a tiger jolted her into action, and she turned and ran as fast as she could. The sudden movement must have triggered an instinct in the tiger, as he shot up the hall in seconds.

Jenny lunged for the doorknob and pulled; it didn't budge. A quick look over her shoulder confirmed the tiger was about to have another snack. He had stopped his run, apparently satisfied his prey was cornered, and he was taking long, confident strides towards her.

He's probably going to play with me until I die. The image her mind conjured gave Jenny the force she needed. She pushed hard on the door one more time, and it opened. Jenny lunged forward as she felt a heavy weight pull down on her backpack. Tony's claws! She screamed and managed to pull her arms—one at a time—out of the strap, still clutching the straps of the bag with one hand, and the door in another, in a deadly game of tug-of-war.

Jenny pulled herself, and the bag, out of the doorway and into the night. She heard the rip of canvas as Tony's claws, apparently caught on a pocket, ripped free. Jenny spun around—one foot away from the tiger—she grabbed the door and slammed it. The bottom of the door caught his paw, essentially stubbing his toe. Tony let out a terrible howl and drew his paw back. Jenny stared at the door; it was partially open, and she could see Tony's face locked in an open-mouthed sneer, fangs stained crimson with Ruben's blood.

She bolted up and threw her weight hard against the door; she heard the click of the latch. She could barely catch her breath as she gulped air and willed her heart to settle. A sudden thud and jolt sent Jenny screaming and running for the truck. She didn't look back.

What if it can open doors? No, no, the tiger can't get out. Just drive, get Zane, and get the hell out of this city.

Jenny threw the torn backpack into the passenger seat, jumped into driver's side, and peeled away, spraying rocks and clumps of dirt everywhere. She drove blindly on the dark dirt road about half a mile before coming to a halt. She hugged the steering wheel. Calm down, she told herself. You're okay.

A hysterical laugh suddenly erupted from her chest, surprising her. Tony got his share ... Ruben ... and she got hers. She had money now. They had money now. She laughed again and stepped on the gas. I'm finally going to leave this place.

When Jenny reached the front gate, a ranch hand name Juarez stopped her. "Where are you headed?" his unshaven face and bloodshot eyes told Jenny he was tired and wishing he was anywhere but here.

"I'm just going to see Zane."

"Ruben actually let you take his truck?"

"My car broke down, and under the circumstances ..." Jenny tailed off and shrugged as if to say, "It is what it is." God, I hope he doesn't check on this, she prayed. She didn't see Mac, and she didn't care right now. "I'm supposed to have it back in a couple of hours."

"I was told to not let anyone in, but Ruben didn't say anything about people leaving," he patted the truck. "I heard what happened to Zane. Man, that is some scary turn of events." Juarez took off his plain blue cap and wiped the sweat from his bald head. Tell Zane I'll say a little prayer for him tonight."

"I will. Thank you." Jenny couldn't help but smile as she drove the truck, and the money, off the compound. I will definitely pray too. I owe God a few hundred thousand prayers at this rate.

Chapter 40:   Mission—Stop an Auction

The ranch, like the sanctuary, was on high ground and was more of a water way than a standing water area. Mac had stayed on the grass as Jenny suggested, and managed to avoid being caked in mud, considering all the rain. After twenty minutes of walking in the humid, mosquito-rich early morning, Mac finally saw the opening Jenny talked about.

It looked like something out of a fairy tale book. A short pathway overarched with trees led to a metal gate totally overgrown with ivy, making it a wall of green. She could even see a peek of Jenny's blue VW Bug, as day light was just starting to break. The clouds had all but disappeared and the heat was making a surprising, revengeful return.

I could just get in the car and go. Maybe the sheriff would believe me and just come look. That would be safer, but I doubt he will believe me in time to catch Clay. I need to get proof, she concluded.

Mac reached the gate. Her hand closed on the cool, dew-laden handle, as she heard what sounded like a dinner bell. Many guest ranches used dinner bells to remind guests when it was time to eat, no matter where they were on the property. It added to the "old Wild West" ambiance.

Mac saw people coming out of, not going into, what she assumed was the kitchen. Clay's men were pointing them to the school house. Damn, what if they are going to the auction now? I have to get a horn now!

Mac took a longing look at her baby blue steed. She could leave now, get the sheriff, and hopefully make it back before the horns disappeared. Heavenly food aromas from breakfast reached her nose—which wasn't helping. Her stomach started to gurgle.

The temptation to leave was overwhelming; then she remembered Keene, lying on the hood of her Jeep with her one night, talking about their future. They talked of Africa and joining a wildlife preservation effort for elephants. They had talked about doing more for the animals, about being more as humans. She was going to keep that dream going. That bastard, Clay, needs to go down for Keene and the rhinos! She was determined to make that happen.

Though her stomach growled in disagreement, Mac crouched down and headed for the back of the building. Looking around the left corner, she got a better view.

In front of the house, immediately to the left and right of the kitchen, were motel room doors. The first door, to the right of the kitchen, had a small metal sign on it that said "Office." To her immediate left, were pens that held pigs, donkeys, chickens, goats, and an ostrich. It reminded Mac of the small petting zoos that accompanied fairs.

Mac recognized the ostrich from two years ago. Her name was Madeline. Mac had met her the day she came here to pick up Keene, after Deputy Allen had him cuffed for sneaking around the property. Luckily, Clay hadn't pressed charges, but he was angry, and while he and Keene debated animal rights, she had stood too close to Madeline's pen and the ostrich had stolen a cap from

214

her head and run off with it. Madeline was quite the trickster.

Mac G.I. Jane'd it, in a crouched walk, closer to the pens. She could see Madeline in the far corner of her pen sneaking the pig's food. She got on bended knee, as if proposing. Her face pressed close to the cool, damp wood of the pen. She looked around, familiarizing herself with her surroundings. Guests appeared to be going to their rooms. Perfect, she thought.

A *thunk* on the head startled her.

"What?" she managed to say softly, while holding her head. It felt like someone had tapped her with the side of her noggin with a cell phone. She looked up, and there stood Madeline with those big lashed eyes and her silly ostrich face.

"Ornery as ever, huh?" she whispered to Madeline, as Madeline stared back at her. "Want to have some real fun?"

Madeline blinked as if responding in Morse code, "Hell, yeah!"

Madeline's gate was similar to horse stalls. It only had a pin that came through the locks. Mac looked for a good moment, next, she pulled the pin and opened the gate. Madeline was quick to run, as if she had waited for this day. She bounced out of her enclosure with zeal, her wings pointing out and her large, round, feathered body bobbing on thin legs in a comical gate.

Mac could see three Asian men, all in dark, conservative suits and ties, walking from the motel rooms. It seemed too early in the day for the men to be dressed so formal on a ranch. Madeline noticed the men too and ran straight for them, her mouth held open in a silent scream of hysteria and wings spread in her earthbound flight. She was fast, and it wasn't long before she was nearly close enough to run one of the men over, before he even caught sight of the bird.

Mac found the realization on the men's face comical. One man separated from the entourage. Madeline followed him.

"Get this thing away from me!" The man yelled and continued to run, as his entourage did nothing to assist him, appearing to enjoy his dilemma, large smiles spreading across their faces.

"Mr. Chen! Just keep running side to side!" One of the ranch hands yelled.

Spouts of what Mac could only assume were Chinese expletives were followed by "Shoot it, shoot it!" in broken English, as Madeline seemed to be in hot pursuit.

Way to pick them Madeline. Mac smiled the smile only karma can grant you, as she remembered Mr. Chen was the one set up to shoot Tony, her furry jail mate.

With all attention on the ostrich, Mac slipped over to the school house. She could hear Clay now.

"Don't touch my Madeline!" More expletives, these ones coming from Clay, and Mac understood each word very clearly.

"Get the hood! Watch her feet!" Clay called out to his ranch hands. "Mr. Chen, run back and forth! She can out run you!"

Mr. Chen bobbed and weaved as Madeline, thrilled with the chase, pecked at his backside, Mr. Chen

216

jumping at each direct hit. Mac smiled and had to cover her mouth to hold in a giggle. She would love to watch more of the hysterical sight, but she knew time was of the essence.

Mac slipped in a side door, finding herself in a short hallway that had four doors, two on each side. They were all open, except one on the very end. The first door led to a small bathroom, the next one to a supply closet. The third door opened into what looked to be an alcoholic's paradise, laid out with liquor and nuts and what Mac assumed was event food. She could only assume the last door led into the auction room. Mac heard voices carrying from a back room ... getting closer quick!

She ducked into the bathroom and locked it. Not a great plan, but the only one I have right now.

Mac heard a door hinge creak, followed by the clomp of several sets of cowboy boots, one pair making the unmistakable clink of spurs.

"Clay said all hands-on deck. Madeline's out," a male voice said chuckling. "Juarez just called me and said we don't want to miss this. It's the funniest thing he's seen in a while."

The door Mac came in opened and closed. She carefully peeked out a small curtained window and could see the empty ostrich pen and several men jogging in various directions, attempting to catch Madeline. She could hear yelling and squawking and stifled another giggle. Madeline must be having a great time!

Knowing her window of time was short, Mac slipped out of the bathroom and made her way to the closed door, putting her ear to it and listened. Hearing no sound, she cracked the door open and peered inside. Mac discovered a large room that had ten, very expensive looking oak arm chairs with deep, brown leather cushions facing a podium. Mac felt disappointment that the needless killing of animals turned such a profit.

On her left, at the front of the room, stood a table with the vases on it, elevated at different levels so all the vases could be seen. Each vase had a tag with a number looped around the base. To the right of the table stood wooden three-panel screens lined up to make a small private walkway to what looked like the top of a door that either led to a closet or more rooms.

Mac ran to the table and picked up a vase. Empty. Damn! She walked towards the panels and followed the short path to the door. Inside was another thin hallway that seemed to go all the way along the back of the building and led to several rooms. Windows faced out at both ends of the hallway. To her right, Mac could see Madeline's pen; to her left, more of the land and other structures.

There were several doors, all open but one. Mac went to the room with the closed door and tried the handle. It was unlocked. She quickly stepped inside.

"Bingo," she whispered.

Inside the room were two folding tables with boxes stacked on top, all big enough to fit each of the vases. All the boxes were numbered and matched the tags she saw in the other room. Mac picked up a box and opened it. Inside sat a beautiful, black horn. A slight smell of dirt and grass wafted up from the box. Mac straightened and looked around. She knew there were too many boxes to carry them all out. Most of the horns were almost the length of her arm making it too awkward to hold in her hands.

She looked for something to carry them in. Seeing nothing, she took off her sweatshirt and fashioned it into a sling-type purse. She quickly rifled through the boxes and grabbed two of the smallest horns. That's all I can carry, she said to herself, but it should be enough to get Clay arrested.

Mac held her precious cargo close to her and headed back the way she came. She found the room still empty and quickly made her way back to the door that led to the closets and bathroom. Glancing through, she saw nothing. She drew closer to the window and saw four big men leading a hooded Madeline into her pen. Thanks, Madeline. I owe you one.

The hood did what it was supposed to do and kept Madeline docile and disoriented. Clay was the one holding Madeline's hood. Mac couldn't hear the words, but he seemed to be coddling and calming her. Mac almost felt sorry for him, seeing how gentle he could be with his pet, but the weight of the horns around her neck reminded her that every evil villain had a pet.

With Mac's escape blocked, she looked for a hiding place. The closet with food and supplies seemed to be her best bet. She went in and closed the door, leaving it open just a crack. She found a corner and sat down, throwing what looked like a tablecloth over her legs.

Mac was curled around the thieved rhino horns as she listened for anything that could verify it was a safe time to leave. She could hear people talking loudly and calling out but couldn't make out their words, except for the ostrich's name. She rested her head on her knees and realized how tired she felt. She had been up all night, and at the moment, she felt safe in the closet.

Mac ran her fingers along the coarse horn, picturing the rhino who once owned it. She had seen pictures of the lifeless bodies of slaughtered rhinos, their horns cut so short only a gaping hole remained in the middle of their faces. She just couldn't wrap her mind around why the world allowed this. More people have to care and realize this is wrong, for anything to change. It's how we overcame slavery, women's oppression, and gay marriage discrimination. It takes a village; no, it takes the majority to change laws and the way people think.

Mac's wandering mind gave way to deeper, dreamier thoughts of how to change the world. I will just rest my eyes. It's going to be at least five or ten minutes before I can move. As Mac closed her eyes, sleep instantly overtook her. She dreamed of fields of dead rhinos, all with their horns missing, their faces bloody.

Chapter 41:   The Get Away

He was ten and playing outside in the backyard. His mom was reading a magazine on a lawn chair. He remembered the warm sun on his face as he looked at his mother. She was beautiful with her long blonde hair tied back in a red bandanna. A cigarette hung from her lips as she flipped through the pages of the magazine. When he looked at her long brown legs, he was concerned at the growing black and blue bruises on the tops of her thighs. Mommy only wore shorts in the backyard.

His mother caught his concern and smiled at him.

"Don't worry pumpkin, it was an accident. They don't hurt. Mommy loves you." Zane's little, boy self smiled, but his smile quickly faltered as he heard a commotion in the house.

"Zane!" His father's voice bellowed out. "How many times have I told you to put away your goddamn toys!" He burst through the backyard.

"Zane! Zane!" He screamed in anger as Zane's mommy jumped up from her chair and got between them, like she always did. Terror filled Zane when he saw his dad's bloodshot eyes as he tried to get past Mommy. A large hand reached out and grabbed Zane's shoulder!

"Zane! Zane! Wake up, Zane!"

" Wha ... !?" Zane shot straight up to a sitting position, and a sharp pain shot through his arm. He touched it and felt the bandages. He wasn't outside. He looked up at his mother; her eyes were concerned. Wait— not my mother. Jenny.

The white room came back into focus. It was a dream … all a bad dream.

***

"Jenny? What's going on?" Zane said; the look in her eyes frightened him.

"It was an accident, Zane. I didn't mean for it to happen!" her voice cracked at the last word, and tears streamed from her eyes and down her tan cheeks.

"What? What happened?" Zane was sitting straight up and fully aware now. He had a better view of Jenny and could see blood on her jeans.

"Oh my God. Are you all right?"

"I'm ... I'm ... I'm okay ... but Ruben. It's all my fault Zane, but it was an accident, and he wouldn't share, but now we can leave. We can leave right now. We have to leave right now!" Jenny's voice was getting loud and panicked.

"Shhhh ... calm down. What are you talking about, Jenny? What happened to Ruben? Wouldn't share what?"

"The money." Jenny replied. "He wouldn't share the money, and I just wanted us to be happy, and I had the key in the tiger's cage, and it jumped and got out and got Ruben, and I ran. It was so awful! He screamed, and I can't get the sound out of my head!" Jenny's words were strung together in one breath and she spoke quickly, but Zane understood every terrifying word.

"Okay, Jenny, what money?" Zane tried his best to be calm, but inside he felt like his entire world just went down the toilet.

"Ruben was taking money from Clay. A lot of money Zane, I mean, like I couldn't even count it all ...

222

there's hundreds of thousands of dollars. I just asked him to split it with us, so we could get away together. He basically told me to go to hell. I was where they put Mac. I had let her go and taken her place. Zane, I'm so sorry, but this has gone too far, and she's my friend. The key was in the lock, and I turned it. I didn't think the tiger would jump, and now Ruben is dead."

Zane's mind was flying over Jenny's ramblings.

"Did you say my brother is dead?" Jenny nodded in response, her eyes welling with tears.

"He was stealing hundreds of thousands of dollars?" Jenny nodded again, her hands clasped in a tight ball under her chin. She looked like a scared child, a child afraid of being punished.

"I ... I ... can't believe he's dead. And what do you mean where they put Mac? I thought they turned her over to the police or something?"

"No! They put her in a cage!"

"Jenny, calm down. You let Mac out to do what?" Zane was about to get out of bed when the unmistakable sound of boots filled the hallway. Jenny was about to reply, but Zane put a finger on her lips.

"Jenny, listen to me. Don't say anything, or just agree with me. Keep it together, and we will leave. Got it?"

If what Jenny said was true, they didn't have much time. Mac would be going to the police, and Jenny killed his brother and stole a ton of cash. Zane hoped his brother had planned on throwing some his way, but he wondered if that were actually the case.

Jenny nodded her head frantically and wiped the tears from her eyes. Zane pulled her close so that the side of her jeans with blood was covered.

Chapter 42:   Going Somewhere?

The footsteps grew louder as Sheriff Moore rounded the corner and entered the room.

"Crap." Zane whispered under his breath.

"Morning, Zane." Sheriff Moore said, with a grin that made Zane's body temperature rise, and his armpits started to sweat. "Oh, and good morning to you, Jenny." The shock in the sheriff's face was unmistakable. "Quite the surprise to see you here, Jenny. It's like finding Juliet Capulet in Romeo Montague's living room."

"You here for a reason, Sheriff?"

"I came to see if you were feeling better. Maybe ready to have a chat?"

"Nothing to talk about, Sheriff. Still feel like I was attacked by a big cat; still feel like you're a jerk." The sheriff's smile waivered but only for a brief second. Zane needed to find a way to get the sheriff out.

"Why, Zane, I thought we were buds. I'm hurt."

Zane said nothing.

"What happened, Zane? You know I think your story is all made up."

"I'm in a hospital bed with teeth marks in my shoulder. Think I'm faking the flu?" Zane was restless and tired of the game. I'm not stupid, he thought. I'm not going to give you anything you don't already know. I've had enough of this small-town bull, and I just need you to leave before Mac finds you.

"No, I believe that part. Was wondering what you knew about Keene."

"Who?" Zane replied, trying to give a convincing look of ignorance.

The smile left the sheriff's face, and Zane could see the switch flip from good cop to bad cop. He probably pushed it too far, but he was tired, he ached all over, and hell, he had a bad night.

"Look, I've had enough of your games." Jenny let out an audible gasp at the change in character. Sheriff Moore took a step closer to the bed and tipped his hat at Jenny.

"Sorry about that, Jenny." He looked back at Zane. "I know both you and Keene were attacked by a cougar, and I know Keene's body was moved to the sanctuary. I just don't really know why someone would do something so stupid. You want to come clean and be helpful? Then I can be helpful to you. Or do want to go down with Clay's sinking ship?"

"Mac's in trouble." Jenny blurted out.

Sheriff Moore froze and turned his head towards Jenny. "What? What about Mac? What kind of trouble? Do you know where she is?"

"I ... got a text a couple of hours ago that she was at Clay's looking around. I was coming to ask Zane what to do. I didn't want her to get into any trouble." Zane watched the sheriff contemplate this.

Zane wasn't expecting the discussion to take this direction, but it seemed to work out for them pretty well.

"All right, I'm going to check this out. Zane, stay put. You're hurt, and I have more questions."

"Does it look like I feel like going anywhere?"

Sheriff Moore walked out. Zane could hear the sheriff start a conversation, probably on his cell phone.

"Give me my clothes, Jenny. Let's get the hell out of here, baby." Zane didn't know how he felt about Jenny right now ... after all, she was partially responsible for killing Ruben, but he'd think about it later, after they got away safely and spent a bit of the money.

Chapter 43: It's Now or Never

Mac was jolted awake by the sound of a door creaking open and two sets of boots clomping on wooden floors.

"Man! That was actually fun!" laughed one of the men.

"Did you see that Asian dude run? That was hilarious! Madeline kept biting his ass!" The men laughed heartily.

Mac pulled in her feet and clutched the horns tightly to her chest. Horror gripped her as the closet door opened. Though her view was blocked by wooden shelves, she saw a large man with his back to her. He wore a blue checkered shirt and reached toward a row of crystal glass decanters full of what Mac could only assume was liquor.

"Want a shot?" blue shirt said to someone out in the hall.

"I guess Clay won't notice a couple of shots missing. What is it?" another man's voice replied.

"Does it matter?" Blue shirt pulled two plastic cups from a pack on the shelf. He popped the top on the decanter, and Mac could hear the slight splash of a drink being poured.

"It's whiskey. Good whiskey." Blue shirt poured two heavy-handed shots.

"Nice," the other man said, stepping closer into the closet. They clinked plastic cups then put them high on the shelf.

"Here." Blue shirt handed the other man a silver platter, placing the decanter and crystal glasses on it. "You get to play sexy waitress, so I'll just call you Jessica, instead of Jess."

"Screw you, Jody. Just because you have a stupid bi-name because your parents didn't know if you'd be gay, doesn't mean you have to give me one."

"You're a bitch, Jessica." The two of them laughed and walked away, shutting the closet door. Mac let out a huge breath she didn't realize she was holding.

Lightheaded, she got to her feet, moving as quickly and quietly as possible. She pressed her ear against the cool wooden door. As she did so, a creak came up from the floorboards, making her freeze in her tracks. She waited, as still as a statue, for a few moments, but she heard no footsteps coming to investigate the noise. Come on Mac, get the hell out of here! she told herself.

With sweaty palms, she placed her hand on the metal knob and opened the door a few cautious inches. Mac looked out at an empty hallway. To the right, coming from within the auction hall, she heard the voices of Jess and Jody. To the left, she no longer heard yelling outside. She slipped through the door and tiptoed over to the window. The grounds were empty. Madeline was in her pen looking pleased with herself. No one was at the side of the house. Mac could see the opening in the fence where the VW was hopefully still waiting.

Okay, everything is clear. I'll slip out and stay close to the house, she planned. It should block me from the view of anyone in the rooms and the office. She slipped out the door, huddled over her sling like an old woman.

Chapter 44:   Auction Time

Clay felt sweat roll down his temples as he walked up the front steps of the school house. I'm putting on too much weight, he thought, as the steps creaked in agreement. Today feels bad. The sooner this auction happens the better. Entering the hall doors, Clay saw Jess and Jody lining up the chairs and the booze on a small table by the aisle. He ran his fingers along the tops of the wooden chairs as he walked to the back offices.

"Hey, boss!" Jody was in his late twenties and had a big, white-teeth grin. His black hair stuck to his forehead, damp from the big ostrich chase. "That sure was a funny sight with Madeline. She looked like she was having the time of her life!" Jess joined in the laughter. He was older—thirty-five—already wearing a cap to hide a hairline that had receded back to the middle of his scalp.

"Madeline had looked comical with her wings spread, eyes wide, beak open at Chen, who looked terrified," Clay chuckled. "Probably, the most fun she's had all year. I mean, how many people have the pleasure of getting chased by an ostrich? I should charge extra for that." They all chortled.

"Did you see him jump when she goosed him!?" Jody added. He and Jess were laughing nonstop now.

"Right! Put a gun in their hands and they are all brave, but one big chicken gets loose and all bets are off!" Jess retorted, his laugh turning into a wheeze.

"Bet he doesn't eat chicken for a week!" Jody remarked, tears now rolling down his face as he wiped them away. "Hey Jess, what's the difference between meat and ostrich?"

"I don't know, man, what?" Jess replied.

"If you choke an ostrich, it dies!" There was a long pause, as Jess's face remained frozen in a punchline smile. A big grin spread across Jody's face at the realization of the dirty joke sank in, and the two burst out in heavy laughter. Even Clay smiled at that one.

"Alright comedians, I'm going to check on things in the back." He looked down at his watch. It was almost eight. Wanting to get this show on the road, he headed towards the back while Jody and Jess shared modified chicken jokes.

"I got one! How does an ostrich kiss his girlfriend?" Jody questioned.

"I don't know." Jess said in anticipation.

"With his pecker!" Jody yelled out, and the pair broke out in uncontrollable laughter as Clay pushed through the rear door.

He headed down the hallway, with an amused smile across his face, to the room that held his meal ticket. This may be my last auction for a while. I should be set after this, he thought, but quickly reminded himself that he had thought that every time. The money he took in at these auctions always motivated him to hold one more.

Clay noticed the door of the storage room wasn't quite shut. He knew he had closed it earlier. He went inside and took a look around. All the boxes sat on the table, but some were slightly askew. That's not right. Not right at all.

Clay reached for the top box of the nearest stack and opened it. A sigh of relief escaped him as he saw the pristine gray horn nestled safely in its silky bed. He opened the top box of another stack … another horn. Chortling at himself for being paranoid, he put the box back. He was going to stop there but decided to check just one more box.

Clay grabbed a box from the bottom of a pile, and as he did, his stomach did an uncomfortable twist—the box was light and felt empty. He shook it like a child with a Christmas gift. He heard a slight sound, like fabric shifting inside. He opened the lid and looked into a box of red silk, with a depression where a horn once lay.

Clay opened all the boxes. Boxes with horns he placed on his left and the empty ones to his right. He counted two horns missing, about half a million dollars' worth. He stood up, feeling anger and the heat of his blood pulsing in his temples. His clenched his fists tightly, nails digging into his palms. He walked out of the little storage room to get Jess and Jody, when he caught a glimpse of a figure through the side window.

Clay quickly covered the distance to the window in long, angry strides. The figure had short, red hair. Clay thought his head would explode as he saw Mac's huddled form making her way outside to a back exit. She had her arms around something. A maddening realization hit Clay.

"My horns," he said through gritted teeth, as she passed Madeline's pen. Blue circles played across Clay's vision, and he had to steady himself as he felt the world turn sideways as the rush of pure anger, at the violation of his property being stolen out from under his very nose, overwhelmed him. Seconds later, his instinct to protect his business, his lifestyle, and his property propelled his feet into action. Clay barreled through to the auction room.

Jody and Jess jumped and then froze, looking at Clay wide-eyed.

"THAT DAMN WOMAN STOLE FROM ME!" Clay yelled at the top of his lungs, his face as red as a beet.

"Wha … what woman?" Jess was stammered.

"Mac! That red-headed devil woman! Come on!" Clay waved them forward into battle. Like a general leading his troops to war, he crashed through the door leading to the side exit and pulled out the gun that had been hanging comfortably in his shoulder holster, waiting for such a moment. He was aware of the enormous pounding his feet made on the wooden floor.

Reaching the outside door, he tried to exit before he had a chance to turn the knob its full turn. Pain exploded on his face as it connected with the door.

Clay felt another surge of anger, followed by a feeling of warm liquid dripping from his nose. He stepped back, wiped his nose, saw blood on his hands, then brought his leg back and gave a mighty kick to the door. Wood splinters flew from it, but it didn't budge. Clay was writhing in anger and kicked it again. The door cracked, but still didn't open.

"Wait, boss!" Jody ran up beside him. Clay stepped back as Jody held up his hands as if being arrested. He quickly moved in front of him, turned the handle, and opened the door.

Clay was breathing heavily. He tried to calm himself, at the realization of trying to kick an unlocked door. Taking deep breaths, he looked for Mac. She was running now, her eyes wide as she looked back at Clay. She reminded him of a deer he shot, right after it tried to get away. Clay stepped out of the house, reached for his gun, and raised it.

"No! Clay!" Jess yelled. "Don't shoot her!" Clay squeezed the trigger and fired. Everyone but Clay instinctively ducked at the sound. The tree to Mac's right sprayed wood splinters. Clay heard a short shout as Mac ducked, one hand instinctively around the stolen property as the other rose in surrender. She fell to her knees. He could shoot her if he really wanted to. She looked like she was trying to get up again.

"Stop running, Mac, or the next one is in your leg! I mean it! I'm done playing hippy games."

Mac rose, one hand still holding his prized horns.

Chapter 45:   Deputy Time

The sun peeked over the horizon, highlighting wispy clouds in pinks and purples, giving the morning a beautiful, red glow. It was already sixty degrees. Going to be a nice one, Deputy Allen thought as he neared Kerrville Hospital. He was happy to have something different to do. With virtually no crime, except for domestic violence and plain ol' country boy tomfoolery, Deputy Allen was bored in his little town. When the sheriff called with instructions to skip the station and head to the hospital to keep an eye on Zane, he was more than happy to do something … anything … different. Plus, he could screw with him.

Deputy Allen had considered leaving Kerrville for several years. His young bride and seven-year-old son were the only reasons keeping him from putting in transfer papers. He wanted more action, like Dallas or even Detroit, but Sara wanted their son Jonathan to grow up in a small town, just like Opie on *The Andy Griffith Show*. She even had an aunt who reminded him of Aunt Bee, except her name was Aunt Caroline. She did, however, make the best pies—which didn't hurt.

It was early—barely eight—when Deputy Allen pulled up to the town's one hospital. The parking lot was empty, except for a white truck pulling out. He parked in the space reserved for emergency vehicles and walked up to the hospital. A fleeting thought of recognition, or what Sheriff Moore called "Spidey sense," flitted across his brain but didn't last long enough for him to figure out why it was there. Deputy Allen felt ice-cold air conditioning hit his face as he walked through the hospital's lobby doors.

Visitors were starting to roll in as the night shift was leaving. He hated hospitals. The smell of ammonia and antibacterial soap, in addition to all of the sick people there, gave him the creeps.

Zane was on the third floor. Deputy Allen reached the elevator and winced in disgust as he pushed the up button, wiping his elevator button finger on the side of his brown uniform pants. When the elevator doors opened, he was happy to see someone dressed in blue scrubs, already in the elevator. That way he wouldn't have to touch the buttons that undoubtedly carried some flesh-eating bacteria.

"Morning. What floor?" the nurse asked.

Deputy Allen noted the male nurse: short ... about 5'6", dirty blond hair, tattoo sleeve on his right arm. He didn't see the man as a threat; noting details about people around him was just something he did. Ever since he was a kid watching *NYPD Blue, L.A. Law,* and *COPS* on TV, he made it a habit to memorize identifying characteristics of everyone he interacted with, as if they were all possible suspects.

"Three, thanks." They rode in silence, which is how the deputy liked it. He hated small talk. Both of the riders avoided eye contact with one another until the doors opened on the third floor. Deputy Allen stepped out of the elevator, onto the white floors, and walked the long hallway. He noted the numbers; the sheriff had told him Zane was in Room 317. Counting in his head as he walked, he noticed a bit of drama at the nurses' desk.

"What do you mean no one is there?" an older female nurse said to a much younger nurse. The older one

236

was plump and had her hands planted firmly on her hips. The younger, a brunette and almost a foot taller, stammered a little.

"I ... I've looked in the bathrooms and on the floor. Maybe he snuck out for a cigarette."

He? That doesn't sound good. That Spidey sense came back, and Deputy Allen quickened his pace down the hallway. He could hear the racket his boots made on the tile floor, and patients who were awake looked through their doors at him as he jogged by.

"Sorry. Sorry for the noise," Deputy Allen said, as he passed rooms three-thirteen and three-fourteen. He was almost jogging now. He dodged a pill cart as a nurse emerged from room three-sixteen.

"Slow down!" a chubby male nurse glared, but his annoyed expression quickly changed to a look of regret when the uniform apparently registered in his brain.

Deputy Allen ran into room three-seventeen and saw a messy, empty bed, white linens scrunched to the bottom. The IV lines dangled and dripped on the floor. A half empty glass of water sat on the tray. No! The white truck was Ruben's!

He smacked his forehead, spun around on his heels, and started to run for the elevator. He grabbed his radio and heard a click. He was about to speak when he realized he had no probable cause to hunt down Zane. Just because the sheriff wanted to talk to a man that got attacked didn't mean he had the right to detain him. He would have to take care of this himself—find the truck and an excuse to pull it over.

Chapter 46:   Final Showdown

Mac was standing, facing away from Clay. Just a breath ago, she had felt a buzz, like a wasp, zip past her ear, and a split second later, the side of a tree next to her exploded in a spray of splintered wood. Then she heard Clay yell at her to stop or he'd shoot her in the leg.

This is it. Game over. Time to stop.

"Put down that damn bag!" Clay's voice sounded furious. Slowly turning and removing the jacket sling, she saw his absolute anger. Clay's face was red, and she could see a vein sticking out on his forehead. Sweat rolled down his face, and the look in his eyes burned into her. The time for standing up for the rhinos was over. It was time to save herself.

"Here! You win. Have your illegal horns." She removed the makeshift sling, pulling it over her head and placed it gently on the ground, then pushed it a few inches away from her with her foot. "Just let me leave!"

Two men, wide-eyed, stood behind Clay. They were the men Mac had heard earlier when she was hiding in the closet. Red and blue shirt … Jody and Jess.

"What's going on, Clay?"

"Shut up, Jess." Jody nudged his friend. Clay didn't look back.

"You got your rhino horns. Now let me go," Mac demanded, but she knew she was kidding herself if she thought it would be that simple. Maybe if I can get Jody and Jess on my side the odds might be more in my favor.

"Did you know your boss was selling illegal horns?"

"Really?" This time it was Jody who spoke. Jess gave Mac a small, knowing smile, as if everyone was in on a joke but her.

"Yes! Lots of them! Worth hundreds of thousands of dollars. Don't you tell your own men about what you do, Clay?" Mac yelled. "Afraid they will expect to be paid more when they find out you've been selling illegal rhino horns?"

Jody and Jess looked at Clay. He didn't turn toward them; he just focused on Mac.

"You boys think you don't get paid enough?" Clay's voice was calm and confident.

"I'm good," Jess replied and looked at Jody.

Jody held up his hands. "No complaints from me, Boss."

Mac lost the little bit of hope she had. She couldn't tell if they knew about Clay's illegal operations or not. But either way, they didn't seem to care. She turned her attention to the spectators that now lined the porch. No one was on their cell calling the police. No one was trying to help her. She felt like she was trapped in a bad dream.

"What is wrong with you people! Call the sheriff! Can't you see this man has a gun pointed at me!" Mac yelled. To her detriment, she noticed there were no other guests *but* the businessmen. Clay must have blocked out the weekend so they wouldn't be interrupted. Realization was beginning to sink in that Clay could actually shoot her, and no one would ever find out.

Mac could see some of the older men in suits whispering to the younger ones, who disappeared back into their rooms. Mac's guess was that they were getting ready to bolt. Hopefully, someone would protect her from Clay.

"We do need to call the sheriff, boss." Jess stated. "We have a trespasser."

"I can't believe this!" Mac heard her own voice, and she sounded like a teenager arguing with a parent, which infuriated her.

Jess met Mac's eyes for the first time during the standoff. "Aren't you the girlfriend of that one boy that was here snooping around last year? The one that stole the white tiger head?"

The mention of Keene hit Mac hard in her gut, and arguments froze in her mouth. Screw this! she suddenly decided. He won't shoot me in front of all these people. Mac immediately darted for the sweatshirt bundle, in one last effort to bolt.

A bullet hit the dirt beside the bag, and Mac jumped back.

"Are you crazy!" She yelled at Clay.

"Stay away from it," Clay said back, his Texas drawl making him sound like a character in an old western movie.

"Goddamn it, Clay! Put the gun in your holster!" Jody yelled.

"Yes, please, Mr. Jones." The voice was accented and calm. It was Mr. Lui. "Shouldn't we have this young lady sit in your office and wait for the police, while we carry out our business?" he continued.

"Mr. Jones, do we have an issue?" One of the younger Asian men spoke this time.

"No issues, Mr. Huang." Clay replied flatly. "We have a thief that is going to delay the antique auction a few minutes, but it's nothing I can't handle. The auction will begin shortly." The men did not move but waited, instead.

Waiting to see what happens to me, Mac thought.

Clay slowly lowered his gun, and Mac could feel the air of tension drop.

"You stay there, Mac. I'm getting what's mine. Jess and Jody can take you into my office."

"That's fine with me," Mac raised her hands and didn't move.

Clay stepped forward and picked up the sling, careful not to drop its contents. He looked up into Mac's eyes.

"Let me just put this back," Clay said, speaking through gritted teeth. Jody and Jess took that as their queue to collect Mac.

"Do you want me to call the authorities?" Jody asked, grabbing Mac's arm.

"Yes. Let's do that! Let's call Sheriff Moore! Pleeeease! Turn me in!" Mac exclaimed. "Let's do it right now, before the auction, huh, Clay? Don't you want to get rid of me?"

Clay pulled his hand radio from its holster on his belt and pressed the talk button.

"Desperado, copy." Static sounded through the radio.

"Dammit, Ruben! Answer me!" Clay yelled into the microphone. Clay shoved the radio back into its holster. "Jody, go to building four ... see if Ruben is there."

"Right," he said but continued to walk towards the office with Mac and Jess.

"Jody, go see about Ruben—now. It's not like him not to pick up. Who knows what else this trespasser has done. I will call the sheriff in a second." Whether it was the look on Clay's face or the need to be away from the mess, Jody gave a salute and jogged to a nearby Jeep, hopped in, and sped off.

Mac was also concerned about why Ruben wasn't here. If he had been sent to the building to check on her, and Jenny was there ... she hoped Jenny was okay.

Maybe she knocked Ruben out. Maybe he knocked her out. What if she was dead? If something happened to Jenny, it will be my fault for making her stay to protect Tony.

Clay tucked the bundle of rhino horns under his arm and headed in the direction of the school house, as Jess led Mac to the office. Mac saw Mr. Lin and two others walking towards Clay.

"Mr. Clay!" As they caught up, they called to Clay, their voices lowered. Before disappearing into the building, she saw Clay and his guests nodding. One of the taller men gave a wave to the others as they headed for the steps. Mac hung her head. No one will get here in time. Clay won't call the sheriff until after he gets rid of the horns, which means this entire hellish night has been for nothing. The rhinos died for nothing. Worst of all, Keene died for nothing.

Chapter 47:   The Show Must Go On

Clay returned the horns Mac stole to their boxes and kept her sweatshirt for an idea he had. He returned to the doorway of the school house just as Mr. Lui, Zhang, Chen, Huang, and Kang-Hu made their way onto the wooden steps, each with a briefcase in his hand, their boots sounding like the clomps of horses walking up trailer ramps. Their companions Wu, Liang, Zhao, and Xing were not with them. Clay assumed they were packing for a quick exit; if not, they should be. Clay allowed the entourage to enter the big room where the chairs were set up.

"Good morning. We will forgo formalities and get right to business." Clay led the buyers to the room where the horns were waiting. He gave a small bow, and the room returned it. "Let's make this simple and brief, gentlemen." He stood by a box and picked it up. "I will go through the sale of each horn, put it in the vase, hand you the shipping box, and you're on your way to get them to a post office or take them on the plane. I have some ranch issues that require my attention and cannot mail them. If you don't purchase them today, it'll be a long time before you have another opportunity."

"What about the girl?" Mr. Huang spoke in a flat business tone, his small brow furrowed, his black hair still sweaty from the morning's fun with Madeline. "Won't she tell the authorities?"

"It's her word against mine. As long as I get these out of here, I have a great many friends in the right places, so she won't be a problem." Clay smiled his big, charming, Texas smile. The men all looked at each other, nodding their agreement to the new terms.

"Mr. Clay, please begin." This was Kang-Hu, the shortest and oldest of the group. With him in, Clay knew the others would be too.

"Great. This first one." Clay picked up the smallest box first, when a muffled *Dukes of Hazzard* theme chimed from his pocket. He clicked ignore, then immediately heard it again.

"I apologize, gentlemen, but excuse me—ranch business, and we are shorthanded." They all looked annoyed at the interruption, especially Mr. Lui. Clay walked just outside the door.

"What's going on, Jody?"

"He's dead, Clay. Somehow the tiger got loose, and he's dead! I walked in and barely got out before the thing took a run at me." Jody's voice was panicked, and his breath was short.

"Calm down. You mean, Ruben is dead?" The bad feeling came back to Clay. "My God, that poor boy." Clay felt a hollow pit in his stomach and a deep sense of loss. I'm the one who sent him over there, he thought guiltily.

"What do I do?" Jody's breath was heavy and quick in the phone, but it was beginning to slow. Clay pushed down his feelings, no time for emotions right now, there would be time for that later. I need to get these people out of here so I can take care of Ruben and Mac.

"Call Frank. He's an expert shot. After Frank kills the tiger, call 911. Don't do it now; I don't want anyone trying to get that tiger out. Just shoot it, and don't touch anything."
244

"Right. One more thing." Jody's voice lowered. "I didn't have a lot of time, but it looks like the safe was open. You were right, boss. Mac took your money, and she probably let the tiger out. Man … Ruben … that poor soul."

"Yeah, I thought so." Clay hung up. Mac doesn't have the money, but she could have hidden it, then let the tiger out. Why would Ruben steal from me? I've been like an uncle to that boy. The two must have made a deal, and then Mac must have tricked him. I'm upset about the money, but I wouldn't ever want Ruben dead. Clay reminded himself the authorities would be here shortly and went back to the auction room.

"Okay, gentlemen, we've had an accident on the ranch. I say we move this along."

Without Ruben, Clay didn't trust the others to help with the actual auction, so he would have to take the money without counting. Not an ideal situation, but he had dealt with most of these men before and never had any issues.

"First horn, gentlemen." Clay slipped on black cloth gloves. He carefully picked up the horn and showed it to the men. "This is our smallest, at 1.5 kilograms. Bidding starts at one-hundred thirty thousand U.S. dollars."

Lui and Chen nodded their heads. Clay knew the older buyers, Zhang and Kang-Hu, would wait for the bigger horns, and the younger buyers would not bid against them. Clay went on.

"One thirty-five."

Lui nodded.

"One forty."

Chen nodded.

"One forty-five." No response from either man. "Gentlemen, may I remind you there will not be another opportunity." Clay knew the horn was worth one-hundred and fifty thousand, but he was willing to let it go for less, in the interest of time.

"One forty-five." Chen said at last, to which Lui bowed out.

This went on for all the horns. Lui, Chen, Zang, and Kang-Hu all purchased both small- and middle-size horns. Zhang and Kang-Hu were bidding on the last and biggest horn.

Clay needed two hands to hold the six-pound horn.

"Since we are short on time, let's start at what it's worth. Three-hundred."

"That isn't how auction works," protested Zhang, but Kang-Hu only nodded, confirming his bid. Zhang looked irritated but joined in the bidding.

"Three-twenty." Zhang said with finality and a prideful look.

"Three-fifty." Kang-Hu spoke calmly. All the men looked at the eldest of the group. Clay felt the excitement of winning the lotto, making all this pain, except for losing Ruben, worth it. Zhang bowed to Kang-Hu, signaling the end.

"Sold, for three hundred fifty thousand dollars." Clay looked at his watch. "Thank you again, gentlemen. I apologize for the rush, but if you could leave your money here, I would suggest a rapid departure. I will make it up to you with a complimentary week-long stay and hunting opportunity at another time of your choosing."

"Thank you, Mr. Jones." Kang-Hu and all the men bowed to Clay. Clay bowed back, and the men quickly gathered their prizes and left behind manila envelopes of cash. Clay waited until they left and didn't go to the safe that was in the room. Instead, he felt along the boards on the wall and pressed an area where only he and his dad knew about.

With a click, he opened a hidden door. He pulled out about twenty thousand from one of the envelopes, then put the rest of it in the hiding place. He took the money and wrapped it in Mac's sweatshirt.

Time to wait for the sheriff.

Chapter 48:   Run, Run, As Fast as you Can

Deputy Allen had just left the hospital when he heard the radio squawk.

"Sheriff Moore. 10-45D. CJ's Exotic Game Ranch. 10-91 tiger, attack. Animal has been put down. Code 2. The deceased is believed to be Ruben Valarez. Copy."

"Moore here. En route." Came the response.

"Deputy, what's your 10-20? Copy." Deputy Allen picked up the mic, pressing the button to respond.

"Five minutes from I-10. Zane took off, I'm trying to catch up. Copy." The radio was quiet for a few seconds. He could almost hear the sheriff thinking.

"Continue pursuit. Bring him in for questioning. Over." That was all he needed to flip on the lights and stamp his foot down on the accelerator. He could feel the grin stretch across his face. This was the action he was looking for. He had taken the only major road leaving the hospital in hopes that they were going to bolt and get to Interstate 10, the first major highway. He was going to be screwed if they went on any of the side roads, let alone the other way on I-10. He was betting on them heading east, towards San Antonio, but he needed more eyes. He reached for the mic and pressed the button to call for help.

"All units. Give me eyes on a white Dodge Ram in the general area of Kerrville. Most likely driven by a white female, about 5'5", blonde hair, blue eyes. Passenger will be a white male, about 5'8", blonde hair. Truck is registered to Clay Jones. Over." As if calling it out invoked it, truck lights materialized in the distance ahead. They must have caught a glimpse of his vehicle lights in
248

the rearview mirror, because they just started to turn off Highway 16 and onto Highway 534, right before the Interstate, and sped up. The deputy turned on his red and blue lights and pursued. The truck didn't slow when the deputy turned onto the 534; instead, it pulled to the side. Chris drove right up to its bumper, the truck in front swaying just a bit, but starting to slow. Chris reached for the speaker's mic.

"PULL OVER," the voice boomed.

This time the truck came to a crawling stop.

"STAY IN YOUR VEHICLE. HANDS ON THE WHEEL." Chris couldn't see the passengers' heads, but they weren't very tall people. He walked up to the side of the truck with his hand on his revolver. Through the heavy tinting, he could see two people and two hands on the steering wheel.

"Open your window, but no sudden movements." He could hear a click, followed by the whirl of the window motor as the glass disappeared into the door.

"What in Sam's hell is your issue, officer?!" an old voice said from the behind the wheel.

"Chris? Christopher Allen? What is this? Some kind of joke?" The deputy relaxed his hand as an old, familiar, cantankerous face filled his view.

"Hi, Mr. Webley." Chris's excitement deflated.

"What? Is that little Christopher?" Mrs. Daisy Webley's sweet voice came from beside the old man as she leaned over to see past her husband. "Why, my goodness! Look at you in your uniform! Your mom must be so proud!" Chris felt hotness in his cheeks, and he felt like he was ten years old again, instead of in his late twenties.

"Why did ya pull me over, boy? You know me. I wasn't speedin'." Grumpy ol' Mr. Webley lived up to his name, but right now Deputy Allen could understand his frustration. He was disappointed at himself for getting too zealous.

"Sorry, sir, I was looking for another truck, and when you sped up, I thought it was yours."

"Hot pursuit, are ya?" He laughed. "Like the movie cops, except this time you caught an old man with a prostate the size of a peach that needs to take a piss!" He gave out a wheezy, phlegmy laugh. "Wait 'til I tell the boys," he said with more wheezed laughter. Chris knew he wouldn't miss Mr. Webley when it was his time to go.

"Now, William. Christopher was just trying to do his job." Daisy smiled at him as she did when he was a boy. She had always come to the rescue of his friends and him when they threw or hit a ball into Mr. Webley's yard. Mr. Webley would shoo them away, but Mrs. Webley would let them in the back door and give them cookies and homemade sweet tea. Decades ago, her hair was long and mostly brown. He remembered thinking she was too nice and pretty for her husband. Now her hair was still long, though almost all grey, but she still smiled like a saint.

"Sorry to keep you, Mrs. Webley." Chris stepped back as Mr. Webley gave a harrumph and pulled away. He could hear Mrs. Webley as they drove off.

"Such a nice boy, don't you think, Willy?"

Embarrassed, the deputy decided to head towards the ranch. He had a BOLO on the truck, so it was only a matter of time before someone spotted it. Thank you, God, I didn't call this in before I pulled them over. I would never have lived that down. He made a mental note to never speak of this to anyone, and hoped that old bastard kept his mouth shut. He went back to the SUV and got on the radio.

"Sheriff, Deputy Allen. I didn't find the truck. En route to the ranch as backup. Over."

"Copy. See you in five."

Chapter 49:   You're Late

The sheriff pulled into Clay's ranch just as several cars were leaving. He managed to note all the drivers, the ones whose windows weren't illegally tinted too dark, were Asian, but he was stopped by one of Clay's ranch hands when he pulled in. It was someone he didn't recognize.

"Hi, Sheriff. Mr. Jones is waiting in his office for you. He has the trespasser." His manners and directness gave the sheriff the impression he was once in the military.

"Is it Mackenzie Williams? Is she hurt?" The sheriff asked. He liked her. He hoped this wasn't at all how it looked.

"I don't know her name, but she is unharmed. Just really needs a shower." The ranch hand waved him through like he had the authority to decide whether or not he would be granted access. This irritated Sheriff Moore, but it was a petty feeling, and he pushed it away. The sheriff pulled up to the buildings. Jody and Jess were waiting on the porch.

Jody looked like he had seen a ghost. Jess looked shaken, but calm.

"Is it true? Is Ruben Valarez dead?" The sheriff put his hand on his belts, hooking his thumb under the leather, his other hand resting on his sidearm as he kept walking towards the men.

"No question on Ruben. God save his soul." Jess was speaking sympathetically. "He did not go out good. Tiger chewed him up like he was a damn cat toy."

Sheriff Moore didn't know if he was the only one to see the irony in an animal killing a human on this ranch.

"It's dead, though—the tiger. Frank put it down." Jody was speaking now, his voice quivering. "We had to be sure Ruben was dead, plus it was loose. Could have killed someone else. Hell, almost got me!"

"That explains the pale look on your face. Where did this happen?"

"Right over in building four." Jody pointed west.

"You say he was out? How would he get out?"

"Sir, I have no idea, but that girl was out here. Clay caught her stealing. I wasn't in the building long, but I noticed the safe was open. Maybe she let him out. Free the animals, and all that crap."

Now this surprised the sheriff. He knew Mac was passionate but didn't peg her as an extremist.

"Deputy Allen should be here soon. Show him and any other emergency vehicles to the scene when they show up. I'll go have a talk with your boss."

Sheriff Moore followed Jess into Clay's office. Clay sat behind his big oak desk, looking like a father wanting to beat his child but trying to remain calm. His face was flushed, but his breathing and eyes were steady. Mac, on the other hand, looked a mess. She was dirty, sweaty, and Steve could see tear streaks through the grime on her face, as well as the look of defeat.

"What in the hell, Mac? Are you all right?" He stepped closer, quickly assessing her for wounds, finding none.

"Of course, *she* is!" The sheriff almost jumped at Clay's outburst, but his training kept him from showing surprise. "Ruben isn't, though. He's dead, and it's all her fault." The sheriff's eyebrows raised.

"Mac?"

"I don't know what happened to Ruben." Mac's voice was angry and defensive. "Clay had put me put in a cage while he had an illegal auction of rhino horns, and Jenny let me out." The sheriff noticed a small flinch from Clay when Mac mentioned Jenny.

"What are you talking about … Jenny who?" Clay's eyes squinted into slits.

"Jenny—Jenny Robertson—I work with her at the rescue. I didn't even see Ruben."

Sheriff Moore looked at Clay for his reaction. Clay let out a huge laugh, leaned back, then shot forward, slamming his hands on his desk.

"LIES!" A bright red color returned to his face.

"Calm down, Clay." Sheriff Moore knew this wasn't going to be easy. "So, you didn't have her in a cage?"

"Oh, I did. I caught her trespassing, and I put her in an empty cage so I could go alert the authorities. She came to steal money from me."

"I did not!" Mac's face was now red and her eyes pleading.

The sheriff held a hand up to silence her.

"Just wait your turn, Mac." He was losing patience with this entire situation.

"I caught her snooping in one of the warehouses, put her in the cage, then came back to ready the antique auction. I left the task of calling the authorities and checking on Mac to Ruben. After that, I didn't see hide nor hair of Ruben for quite a while and couldn't raise him on the radio either. Then I caught this one trying to run away with my cash." Clay brought out Mac's sweatshirt, untied it, and dumped out a small fortune in bills. Mac's eyes widened at the money.

"That's when I sent Jody to check on Ruben. She must have set the tiger loose on poor Ruben, then robbed me. You should be ashamed, Mac! Ruben didn't deserve to die like that." Clay's eyes looked accusingly at her.

Mac was still staring at the money, her mouth agape. It looked like she was trying to speak, but she could only manage stutters.

"As soon as I found out what happened to Ruben," Clay continued, "I had Jody call the authorities. I don't need any issues. These kids have been nothing but trouble. I'm just trying to run a business here."

"Mac? You have a different story? Were you trespassing?"

"I was looking for clues."

"Clues for what?"

"Clues about Keene."

"That's for the police to investigate, Mac. Are you a detective now? Watched a lot of NCIS? Stayed in a Holiday Inn Express?" Sheriff Moore hated all cop shows that made people think they could do better than the real police.

"What? No! I ... I didn't trust you. You were blaming *me,* so I came here. *You* weren't doing anything! You don't know anything!" Sheriff Moore's blood came to a rapid boil.

"I've had just about enough of your foolish, extreme actions." Sheriff Moore was starting to see Mac in a less than favorable way. She seemed reckless. "Is this the first time you've been here, Mac? Maybe you came with Keene, and when he got mauled, you took him back to the enclosure at the sanctuary."

"What? No!" Mac yelled. "I came here and found rhino horns that Clay sold to those Asian guys! That's why Keene is dead!"

"Rhino horns?" the sheriff asked, looking at Clay, "You got any rhinos on your property, Clay?"

"Nope. Closest thing I have to that kind of wildlife is some wildebeest."

"Keene was attacked by a cougar, Mac, not a rhino."

"Zane!" Mac's eyes glowed. "Zane was attacked by a cougar when they were chasing me."

"Zane saved her life, Sheriff. That boy should get a damn medal. She went into a dangerous enclosure, and Zane went to protect her."

Sheriff Moore noticed Clay was calmer now, fingers laced on the desk. Mac, on the other hand, looked enraged. She reminded him of his teenage niece, when she would get in trouble for things that were never her fault.

"Jenny … Jenny let me out of the cage. I left to get the horns. Where is Jenny? She must know something. Is she okay?"

"Mac." The sheriff softened his tone to try and help calm her down. "I saw Jenny at the hospital with Zane."

"She probably went there after she let me out. I told her to watch Tony, so he didn't get shot."

"Tony?" Sheriff Moore looked at Clay. Clay shrugged.

"That's the tiger's name." Mac said matter-of-factly.

"That tiger would have been a new attraction. We don't shoot that type of game here. It's not illegal to own tigers and I have him registered." Clay replied flatly.

"You heartless ..." Mac managed to say, through gritted teeth.

"Mac, I think we need to continue this at the station. Mr. Jones, I will need a formal statement. If you could come to the station as soon as you can today."

"Of course, Sheriff." Clay stood to walk out the door with them. "I need to contact Ruben's family first, though. God rest his soul. Awful shame how he died. That boy was like a son to me."

Sheriff Moore motioned Mac towards the door.

"I should cuff you, but I trust I won't have any more issues with you," he said. Mac, head down, got up and walked out. He gently placed a hand at her elbow to let her know she wasn't free.

As the sheriff and Mac walked to the patrol SUV, he read Mac her Miranda Rights. Mac was silent all the way through. It seemed she had no more to say. He opened the back door, and she climbed in, glaring back at Clay. Clay, stood in the doorway with no expression in return.

"Thanks again, Sheriff. Hopefully, this animal nonsense is all over."

"I'm pretty sure you won't get any trouble from Mac for a while." He got in the cruiser and picked up the mic.

"Chris, I got Mac. She's safe. Bringing her to the station. Be back to assist."

"Copy. Glad she's okay."

The sheriff looked back at Mac. She was staring out the window. He could see tears falling from her eyes as she sniffed and wiped her nose with her sleeve.

"Me too," he said into the mic, and meant it. He didn't know what was going on with her, but he was glad she was physically okay.

Chapter 50:   Nobody Knows the Troubles I've Seen

Mac felt a pull from a world that was blurred and dark. She sensed she was somewhere strange. I'm not home in my bed in the trailer, her half-conscious self sensed. With her eyes still closed, she tried to remember where she was, but she knew she didn't want to. Her hip felt cold and ached; she was on a hard surface. Images of running between trees and the face of a tiger filled her brain.

Sounds of muffled talking entered her consciousness. A bright light seeped through her eyelids. She cracked one eye. A brick wall, painted thick in cream paint, filled her view. The wall reminded her of the inside of her high school classrooms. Where am I? A few more blinks told her she was lying on her side on a very uncomfortable bench. She rolled gingerly onto her back, as every muscle and bone in her body ached. A groan escaped her as she stared up at incandescent lighting. I'm in jail, came the flat reply from her mind.

"Good morning," said a male voice.

Mac looked around as the cell melted into the reality of the hell she was in. It all came flooding back: the chase, the cage, the tiger, the horns, Jenny, and Ruben. Ruben is dead, and it's my fault. She tilted her head to see the deputy behind a desk.

"Lucky you, you got a cell to yourself. The guys aren't that lucky. Few of them have to share, but this isn't the Holiday Inn."

Mac stared back at the ceiling. She was screwed. She had ruined her life in one night. She was going to jail,

Clay got away with selling the horns, and Tony and Ruben were dead. She never liked Ruben, but she did not mean to get him killed. She didn't want anything to die. And what about Jenny? Maybe she could help, but Mac doubted it. If she was the one who let Tony out, she was probably long gone or would lie about it. Mac instinctively reached for her pockets. She didn't feel the rectangle shape anywhere.

"Where's my phone?" Mac sat up.

"You didn't have one." Deputy Allen looked up from some paperwork and crossed his hands.

"Dang it." Mac said to herself as she remembered Clay had her phone.

"Don't worry, we'll let you call a lawyer and maybe your mom. It's a small town. We can afford two calls," Deputy Allen answered.

Mac considered telling him Clay had her phone, and she had pictures of the rhino horns, but she doubted he would believe her. She was pretty sure Clay would destroy it, if he hadn't already.

"What time is it?"

"It's noon. You've been out for a couple of hours." He stood and walked to the cell. "Ready for some food?" Mac wanted to say no, or screw you, but the rumble in her stomach disagreed."

"I'm vegan."

A chuckle escaped him. "I'm Catholic, but I will see what I can find you."

After a short time, Deputy Allen came back with a banana, bread, canned green beans, Oreos, and apple juice. "Best I could do. It's Texas, even the veggies are made with meat."

"Anything would probably taste good right now. I'm starving. And I appreciate the effort." Mac ate the plate clean and asked for two more bottles of apple juice.

Her belly full, she sat with her back against the wall and looked at the cell. She was behind bars again, and who knew for how long. Tears started to roll down her cheeks. When she wiped them from her face, she saw they were dirty. She looked down at her filthy clothes. When did I last have a shower? She struggled to remember anything after leaving the ranch, but all she could recall is that she was tired, and the sheriff said she could rest a bit. They hadn't even fingerprinted her yet.

With the adrenaline now gone, Mac felt defeated and sore. She cupped her hands and cried into them. They smelled of dirt and sweat. She could even smell the earthiness of the horn she had held in her hands.

I've failed Keene. All those rhinos were brutally killed for profit, and no justice came of it. People had died because of the horns, and still no one would listen. Mac lifted her head at the sound of a click of the door, wiping her nose in her shirt and her tears away from her face. The sheriff walked in.

"What's going to happen to me?"

"In general?" the sheriff's joke fell flat to Mac's ears.

"This isn't funny. Clay Jones is getting away with murder, I don't know where Jenny is, and about a million dollars in rhino horns just left the country."

"That's a pretty fair estimate." The voice came from behind the sheriff. Mac immediately recognized him.

Mr. Lui! But did he just speak without an accent?

"What? You! You were there!" Mac quickly stood, anger lighting up her face.

"Hold on, Mac. Mr. Lui is here to help you." The sheriff walked towards the cell and opened it. Mac looked at the pair, confused and leery of the freedom she was being offered.

"Miss Williams, I am Kenji Mori." Kenji pulled a badge from his inner suit jacket pocket. "I'm an undercover investigator with the Wildlife Justice Commission. I was posing as a buyer for the auction on Clay Jones's property. I am working with the U.S. Fish & Wildlife Service to break up an international smuggling ring that has targeted some of the world's most endangered animals … more specifically, the rhino horn and elephant ivory trade."

"You knew he was dealing in the horns? You got him?"

"He is being arrested as we speak," the sheriff added. "Deputy Allen went there with more WJC agents, not long after you ate."

"But, why didn't you say something?!"

"I was undercover, and when I saw you, you weren't in danger." Kenji put his badge back in his jacket. "I got here as quickly as I could without tipping off the buyers."

"But you *saw* me." Mac said, thumping her hands to her chest. "You saw Clay point a gun at me!"

"I had my gun. If it escalated any more, I would have done something. Mac, this undercover operation has taken almost two years. I had to be cautious."

"Mac, Clay doesn't kill people, but that's not true of most of the people who orchestrate these auctions—you were actually lucky it was Clay," Sheriff Moore added. Mac looked at the sheriff in disbelief.

"This is true." Kenji added. "Most of the actual hunters are poor, destitute Africans who are trying to feed their families and are promised money for the horns. When they deliver, they find that the payoff is usually much less than they were promised, and sometimes the hunters are shot as well. The rhinos aren't the only victims. The poor and weak minded are as well. This business comes with all the same dangers as the drug trade." Kenji handed Mac a card. "As far as Clay, he's just one of the many suppliers. We are hoping to get more information to lead us to someone farther up in the hierarchy. He's what you would call *small potatoes*."

"But what about the buyers? Where are the horns? Who did Clay get them from? Where's Jenny? What happened to Ruben?"

"As far as your horn questions, I'm not at liberty to say, as it is an active investigation. I can only say that people have been apprehended. Thanks to you, that includes all those involved in the auction."

"Why thanks to me?" Mac replied.

"The way the auction was going to go down, there was a chance we wouldn't be able to get all the players with the horns. If we would have raided the auction, the buyers could have pleaded that they were only buying vases. If the packages were mailed out, no one would have the actual horns on them, but with you speeding up the auction, we caught everyone with the evidence."

"So, these horns … are they actually worth all that money? I mean, they *are* just horns." The sheriff asked, sounding skeptical.

"Yes. It's actually becoming more profitable then smuggling drugs. The Chinese use the horns for traditional medicine; some believe they can heal cancer. Others display them as a sign of success and wealth."

"It's insane people put so much value on those horns. Waste of an animal as well." Sheriff Moore said, sounding unimpressed.

"Yes, it is a senseless act. More than seven thousand African rhinos have been lost to poaching since 2007. There are about twenty-five thousand left in Africa, only thirty thousand in the entire world. At the rate of poaching, rhinos could be extinct in three decades or less. That is why we are taking poaching very seriously and are trying to put an end to these illegal auctions."

"Mac," Kenji continued, "I do appreciate your bravery. If you would be interested in pursuing a more active, but safer role in the protection of rhinos, there are conservation field programs or environmental education programs I can point you to. Just getting the word out and raising funds to support the communities in Africa that protect the rhinos is a tremendous help. We could always use someone with your perseverance and passion." He gave the slightest smile before quickly turning to leave.

"Thank you, Sheriff. My agency will be in touch. I will see myself out." Kenji exited the room. Mac pocketed his card.

"So, I'm—"

"Free to go." The sheriff finished Mac's sentence. "I can take you back to your home," Sheriff Moore said and started to lead her out of her cell, then the station.

"... and Jenny and Zane left together," the sheriff said after a few moments.

"Jenny and Zane left where?"

"Don't know yet, but they won't get far with a BOLO out." Mac knew, from watching way too much CSI, that BOLO meant "be on the lookout." Sheriff Moore opened the outside door to the parking lot. Mac was immediately assaulted with the extreme heat and humidity of South-Central Texas—she never felt so appreciative of it until now.

"But what happened with Tony ... the tiger?" Mac was confused at this. "Who let him out of the cell?"

"We don't really know. Could have been an accident. Jenny may or may not have been there. Clay hasn't said anything about money being stolen, aside from the money he claimed you took." They approached his patrol SUV. He opened the passenger door. Mac stepped inside and was relieved she didn't have to sit in the back again.

"So, what happens to Jenny?" Mac was at least relieved to know Jenny wasn't found dead with Ruben but had to wonder, if she hadn't told Jenny to stay, would Ruben still be alive?

"We won't know the details till we catch up to Bonnie and Clyde and hear Jenny's side of the story—if she was even there. I can't see Ruben doing it." The sheriff shook his head sadly. He's been around dangerous animals for too many years to be careless, but it only takes once."

Mac had a feeling Jenny took the money, but she wasn't going to say anything. Was Jenny really that desperate? Mac couldn't even guess at this point. She didn't seem to know Jenny at all, except that she did come to save her, so maybe at least part of their friendship wasn't a lie.

Despite their differences, Mac hoped Jenny would be alright.

***

An hour later, Mac was in the hottest, longest shower of her life.

Chapter 51:   After the Moment has Passed

It had been a month since the auction. Mac slept for an entire day and night after the sheriff brought her back to her too quiet trailer. Within a few days, she was quickly back into the hurried routine of the sanctuary. Mac kept herself busy, volunteering for extra shifts, working until exhaustion. Over the last month she felt lonely and hollow. She felt she didn't have a path or purpose without Keene by her side. They always supported and encouraged one another. Now she had no one to share her life and passion with ... at least not like she had with Keene. She had turned in her notice to Nancy and was going to move back with her parents for a while. She only had three days left, and she still had no idea what to do.

It was 3 p.m.. Mac decided to take a break and went to watch Xena and Thor. She did this every day now. She took this time to think of Keene and in a way, to talk to him. She felt she understood him more now ... why he took so many chances and went to such great lengths. Knowing what was going on in the world, she felt she had outgrown J.A.W.S. and wanted to do more, but how much more could one person do alone? I wish you were here. I miss you. I need you, Keene.

A car door closed from up the hill behind her. Mac turned to see Sheriff Moore walking down towards her, with a wave.

"Mac. How have you been?"

"Just peachy," Mac said, with a wave and a flat tone.

"I figured I should let you know that Clay's been charged with illegal trade."

"You could have called." Mac knew she was being mean, but she couldn't help herself.

"Yeah, I could have, but I wanted to see how you were, and I didn't think this was phone call material."

"Is that all he's being charged with? What about Keene? He moved his body."

"He didn't." the sheriff paused. "He's saying he didn't know anything about it. Of course, Ruben can't tell us anything."

"What about Zane? What did he say? I heard him and Jenny were caught in Louisiana."

"Seems Zane and Clay formed some kind of pact. Same lawyer, hired by Clay, so the story told is that Ruben moved Keene; afraid he'd lose his job or something over someone being attacked in the pens." the sheriff said, matter-of-factly. "The more support Clay gets from Zane, the lesser the charges. Right now, Clay is looking at twenty-four to thirty-six months in prison, and he owes, respectively, about fifty thousand dollars in fines, penalties and goods to the government."

"That's it? Three years for murdering rhinos?"

"And fifty thousand dollars. That's not chump change, and the money actually goes to programs to help the rhinos. Kenji told me that."

"That's a drop in the bucket for a man like Clay. Doesn't feel like justice." Mac sighed.

"I don't know, Mac. I think jail time and high fines make people think twice for a knickknack in their office. Also, I'm sure the IRS is going to take a closer look at his finances now. Wouldn't surprise me if he ends up getting more penalties."

"I guess you're right." Mac crossed her arms. "What about Jenny and the tiger?"

"Well," the Sheriff let out a long breath. "From what Jenny told me, Ruben tried to attack her. She stated she accidentally let the tiger out. She also stated she picked up the money with intentions to give it back; Clay didn't press charges."

"I feel like it's my fault Ruben was attacked."

"How do you figure that?" Sheriff Moore asked.

"I'm the one who told Jenny to stay behind with Tony." Mac felt the heat of tears threaten to fall. "What if she is somehow responsible for letting the tiger out?"

"Look, any way you slice it, that is not your fault. You can't hold yourself accountable for other people's actions." Sheriff Moore stepped closer and looked her in the eyes. "Yes, you were on Clay's property, but he shouldn't have put you in that cage. It's an unfortunate chain of actions. Anyway, just thought I'd let you know the outcome. You take care, Mac." The sheriff tipped his hat and turned, walking back to the patrol SUV. Mac headed back to her trailer.

***

A tall, handsome man in a sleek blue suit stood at Mac's trailer door. He looked oddly familiar as he stepped forward, hand out.

"Hi, I'm Donavan. I'm Keene's uncle." Mac shook his outstretched hand.

"Well, that explains it." Mac replied as she eyed him up and down.

"Explains what?" Donavan replied with one eyebrow up in a quizzical look.

"Oh, it's just you looked familiar to me, and now I know why." She focused on his green eyes. "You look very much like Keene."

"Yes. People usually mistake us for father and son." Mac could see pain behind Donavan's face as he spoke. "Unfortunately, his father passed away some time ago. May I sit down? I have some documents for you, from Keene."

"Oh, um sure." Donavan stepped aside as Mac opened the door. He held the door for her as she walked in. His polite manner didn't escape her attention. Mac sat at the table as Donavan joined her. He placed a briefcase on the table, unlatched it, and pulled out a manila folder.

"Miss Mac." Donavan paused and looked at her, holding the folder to his chest. "Keene was very passionate about animal rights, the environment, and human rights. He also was very passionate about you. On his last visit home, he left a few things with me for my safekeeping. One—" Donavan opened the envelope and brought out a thick set of documents. "—one is this. Keene felt, if something happened to him, he wanted someone to be able to help the animals. He wanted that someone to be you. As you know, it takes more than a village to do any good in this world; it takes money."

Mac took the documents and scanned the first page. Her eyes widened. "What—is this real?" She asked, unsure she read the document correctly.

"Yes, Keene had a trust fund, set up for him by his father. It is now yours. I will be your financial executor and will write the checks for you to help animals and live comfortably. He said he wanted to give you funds to do whatever you wanted. He trusted that you would make the right choices. I'm just here to help … as finances with such a large sum of money can be overwhelming."

"Large sum. Yes, this is a large sum." Mac was overwhelmed with the idea that Keene was still taking care of her, even from beyond his life. "I don't know what to say. I can't believe he did this ... he was always so incredible, and generous. I'm just so overwhelmed he had that much confidence in me." Mac felt a tear roll down her check.

"Yes. Well, he was more than confident." Donavan reached into his briefcase and pulled out a black velvet box and slid it in front of her. She froze, terrified of what might be in the box and the pain that would come with opening it.

"What is it?" her voice wavered.

"I think it would be better if you opened it." Donavan looked at Mac with sympathetic eyes.

Mac slowly opened the box with shaking hands. A silver band lay on a small, velvet pillow. Little elephants, holding each other's tails in a caravan, were etched in a circle around the band. All the elephants had tiny diamonds for eyes. Mac couldn't stop the volcano of pain that rose in her heart, like hot lava. She looked at Donavan. He took her hands and held them.

"He said he was going to ask you to marry him. I was holding the ring for the right time. I'm sorry Mac."

"I am too." Mac said, barely a whisper, as the sobs that followed were heavy, and could be held back no longer. Donavan drew Mac into him in a fatherly hug and held her tight. He let her sob. Mac was thankful that he didn't say, "It will be alright," or "He's in a better place." She would trade any of this for him.

"He's dead, and it's not fair, and life sucks!" She cried. Donavan embraced her tighter.

"I agree. It does suck, and it's not fair. I'm so sorry to make you cry, but I know Keene wanted you to have the ring." He let her go and handed her tissues from his pocket.

Mac could feel the snot threaten to drip down her face like an unkept toddler. She took the offered tissues and blew her nose.

"I have to go." Mac noticed Donavan's eyes were red and threatening tears also. "I will contact you tomorrow, but please call me if you need anything. All my contact information is on this card." He pulled a business card from his jacket pocket and slid it over to Mac. She picked it up and stared at it.

"Thank you." Mac said. She felt drained, tired; she did not get up as Donavan let himself out.

Mac sat, still staring at his card. She picked up the ring from its pillow bed and placed it on her wedding finger. Tears overflowed the rim of her eyes, she absently wiped at them while she turned the ring around and around, watching the elephants walk in an eternal caravan around her finger.

"Call me if you want to do more," that was the same thing Kenji had said to her before she left the police station.

Mac felt a wash of resolve rush through her body, an idea of what she was going to do. Before she met Keene, she was happy to spend the rest of her life at the J.A.W.S., helping the local animals. Now, she saw the bigger picture Keene saw. She also understood that *one* person can make a difference, and *she* wanted to make a difference—for Keene and for herself.

Mac ran to her room and packed her bags. She threw everything into the Jeep and was about to leave when she remembered someone. She went into the supply and food barn and grabbed everything she needed. She'd send a nice sized donation later to cover it all, now that she had the funds. With an animal kennel in hand, she walked over to the small animal enclosures.

"Hey, Fenny," Mac said softly as she opened the door and laid the carrier on the floor. Fenny ran happily into it. Mac reflected again on the night she and Keene shared with Fenny. She smiled as she remembered the giggles and the looks in each other's eyes. Keene had kissed her in here—a long, loving, passionate kiss that made her think they would be together forever.

Mac lifted the kennel so she could peer inside. Fenny's big brown eyes stared back at her, and his equally big ears focused on her direction. He licked his lips in excited anticipation. In a way, with Fenny by her side, Keene would still be with her, for a little longer. "Let's go to Africa little one."

--- The End--

Look for more adventures with Mac in my upcoming novel, where she travels to Africa and finds herself in the middle of an ivory trafficking war. On one side, park rangers and conservationist, on the other, poachers and the network lords that paid for the animals' slaughter.

Don't miss ***Elephant War!***

Acknowledgements

Thanks to my friends James, Stephen, JP, Jack, Brian, and Joseph, who have read every word more than once. Thank you to my editor Lisa Brown and technical advisors Catherine DeYoung and Lori Diseati.

#